PRAISE FOR THE REAL REBECCA

'Our new Book of the Week is *The Real Rebecca* by Anna Carey, a great new voice and definite Princess of Teen.'

Books for Keeps

'I laughed and squirmed my way through *The Real Rebecca*, the sparkling and spookily accurate diary of a Dublin teenager. It's stonkingly good and I haven't laughed so much since reading Louise Rennison. Teenage girls (and grown-up teens) will love Rebecca to bits!'

Sarah Webb, author of the *Ask Amy Green* books

'This book is fantastic! Rebecca is sweet, funny and down-to-earth, and I adored her friends, her quirky parents, her changeable but ultimately loving older sister and the swoonworthy Paperboy.'

Chicklish Blog

'What is it like inside the mind of a teenage girl? It's a strange, confused and frustrated place, as Anna Carey's first novel *The Real Rebecca* makes clear ... A laugh-out-loud story of a fourteen-year-old girl, Rebecca Rafferty.'

Hot Press

'The story rattles along at a glorious rate – with plenty of witty asides. Rebecca herself is a thoroughly likeable heroine – angsty and mixed-up but warm-hearted and feisty.'

Books Ireland

'Carey's teen voice is spot-on ...'

Irish Independent

PRAISE FOR REBECCA'S RULES

'A gorgeous book! ... so funny, sweet, bright. I loved it.'

Marian Keyes

'Amusing from the first page ... better than Adrian Mole! ... highly recommended.'

lovereading4kids.co.uk

'The teen voice is spot on. Carey captures the excitement, camaraderie and tensions brilliantly.'

Books for Keeps

'John Kowalski is an inspired creation.'

Irish Independent

'Sure to be a favourite with fans of authors such as Sarah Webb and Judi Curtin.'

Children's Books Ireland's Recommended Reads 2012

Anna Carey is a freelance journalist from Drumcondra in Dublin who has written for the *Irish Times*, *Irish Independent* and many other publications. Anna joined her first band when she was fifteen and went on to sing and play with several bands over the next fifteen years. Her last band, El Diablo, released two albums and toured all over the country. Her first book, *The Real Rebecca*, was published in 2011, and, to her great surprise, it went on to win the Senior Children's Book prize at the Irish Book Awards. To the delight of many readers, Rebecca returned in the critically acclaimed *Rebecca's Rules*, which was shortlisted for the same prize in 2012 (she didn't win this time, though).

Anna Carey

Irish Book Award Winner

THE O'BRIEN PRESS
DUBLIN

First published 2013 by The O'Brien Press Ltd,
12 Terenure Road East, Rathgar, Dublin 6, Ireland.
Tel: +353 1 4923333; Fax: +353 1 4922777
E-mail: books@obrien.ie
Website: www.obrien.ie

ISBN: 978-1-84717-564-9

1 2 3 4 5 6 7 8 9 10
13 14 15 16 17

Layout and design: The O'Brien Press Ltd.
Cover illustrations: Chris Judge
Printed and bound by CPI Group (UK) Ltd, Croydon, CR0 4YY
The paper in this book is produced using pulp from
managed forests.

The O'Brien Press receives assistance from

ACKNOWLEDGEMENTS

Thanks to everyone at the O'Brien Press, especially Clare Kelly, Brenda Boyne and, of course, my patient editor Susan Houlden; Chris Judge for another fantastic cover; Sarah Webb and Sarra Manning for their continued support; the lovely Marian Keyes for her much-appreciated kind words; the extended Carey and Freyne families, especially Lisa and Eli, aka the Meeper, who cheered me greatly when I was writing this book; everyone on Twitter who distracted, cheered and amused me while I wrote; Maria Doyle Kennedy, Rebecca Moses and Dara Higgins for their excellent band name suggestions; and, of course, my husband Patrick Freyne, who always made me laugh when I was in the creative doldrums. And a very special thank you to Michael Barron and Gerard Roe who do such amazing work at BelongTo, and to all the smart, hilarious Ladybirds who shared their stories with me. If I got anything wrong, it's my fault. I hope they like the book.

To Helen, without whom Rebecca would (probably)

never have existed at all

MONDAY ☺

I'm not meant to be writing this.

I'm meant to be studying, because our summer tests are in just three weeks, and my mother has locked me in my room and forced me to do maths and geography for an hour. Well, okay, she hasn't literally locked me in my room. But this is probably only because my room doesn't actually have a lock. I wish it did, though, then I could lock her out. She keeps peering in and making sure I'm studying. And she says reading non-school books doesn't count, even though I tried to tell her that all reading is the study of literature and that I was learning about LIFE and art, but she didn't care. She knows there's no chance I could be on the Internet or the phone because I don't have a computer of my own and she has taken my phone away and locked it in her study! Not that it would be much use, I have no credit on it anyway.

But still, Cass or Alice might ring me. Although they probably won't; their parents have got all strict about studying and homework too, so I bet they're locked (not literally) in their rooms as well. Recently all our parents have started saying annoying things like: 'You've got up to an awful lot over this school year, but school still has to come first!' Cass's mum even started hinting that if she doesn't do well in the summer tests, she might have to go to a special summer school where she would have non-stop maths grinds. This is a terrible prospect for poor old Cass and, on a selfish note, would totally spoil all our big summer plans.

Our parents are right about some things, though. Not about possibly forcing Cass to go to summer maths classes, of course, but it's true, a lot did happen this year. Nothing really happened at all when we were in First Year, apart from the time Ellie fell into the lake on the school tour to Glendalough, of course, but our second year at St Dominic's has been surprisingly dramatic. I mean, first my mum wrote that terrible book and everyone thought it was about me, and then I met Paperboy, the nicest boy in the world, and then me and Cass and Alice started our band, and then Paperboy moved to Canada and I was a miserable hollow shell of a girl for months and months.

All that on its own would have been eventful enough – much more eventful than all of First Year – but then we had to go to crazy Vanessa's giant birthday party and Alice had her accident so the band had to go on hiatus. And THEN we were in the school musical and I met John Kowalski and went temporarily insane for a few weeks (it is the only explanation for the fact that I thought he was a decent human being). And then we did the musical. And since then we have been doing band practices and planning for the greatest musical summer ever.

I have to admit that from the outside it might look as if we have not had much time for studying and all that. But that would be very unfair. My parents have clearly forgotten that when I was rehearsing for the greatest school production of *Mary Poppins* ever, they were obsessed with my homework and kept forcing me to stay at home and study practically every non-rehearsal night and at the weekends too. And when I was all miserable about Paperboy going to Canada, I sometimes ended up just doing my homework by accident because after a while anything was better than staring out the window for hours wondering why he hadn't mailed me in ten days. So, actually, all our extra-curricular activities haven't made any difference to my school work at all.

Of course, there's no point in telling my parents any of this because they never listen to me. This is because they're totally obsessed with their latest plan to humiliate me in front of the world. But I can't bear to write about that now, it's too terrible.

Oh no, I can hear Mum coming up the stairs to check on me AGAIN. Better go.

TUESDAY ☾

I can't wait for these stupid summer tests to be over. I keep dreaming of being able to just lie around and read and not have to think about maths or Irish. I actually can't remember what it was like not having to study all the time. It's like having school twenty-four hours a day. Speaking of which, actual school is even worse than ever, because all our teachers are acting like we're doing our Leaving Cert rather than our second-year summer exams, which, let's face it, are not going to make any difference to our lives whatsoever. I think some of them are still annoyed with us musical people for spending so much time on *Mary Poppins*. Miss Kelly can't stop going on about it in geography class (when she's not telling us about environmental disasters, her favourite subject).

'Now, some of you may have been too busy singing and dancing to notice,' she said this afternoon after going on about climate-related crop failure for what seemed like about ten years, 'but we did actually cover this subject a few months ago.'

Even Mrs Harrington has started to have little digs at us in English class, and she was quite enthusiastic about the whole musical thing when we were doing it.

'I know some of you have had lots of fun and games this year,' she said, 'but we need to get down to work now and make up for all that lost time!'

I don't know what they're talking about – it's not like we got out of lessons when we were doing the musical. Apart from the day of the actual show, but even that was just for a few hours.

'I think doing the musical should count as an exam,' said Cass when we were walking home. 'Or even two exams. I mean, we worked really hard on something and it turned out brilliantly. And we learned loads. Like, I learned how to make sets, and you learned lots of songs and how to perform them, and we all learned how to put on a big show. I think we should get off at least one exam for having done all that.'

I think she is right. But unfortunately neither our school nor our parents agree on the importance of all our hard work. Which is pretty hypocritical of my parents, because now they're off doing a musical of their own, and they make such a fuss about it you'd think they were taking part in a big Broadway spectacular rather than something that's going to be put on in a school hall down the road. Yes, my own musical adventures reminded them of the time they took part in some crazy college production of *The Pirates of Penzance,* and they went off and found a local musical society to join. So now they are both going to star in a production of *Oliver!,* which I hope I can get out of going to see because the last thing I need, after the year I've had, is being forced to watch my parents dressed in Victorian outfits singing about food glorious food. But I bet I'll end up going whether I like it or not, and, knowing my luck, someone from my class like Karen Rodgers will be there too, and I'll never hear the end of it. This may seem unlikely, but after all the embarrassing things my parents have got up to this year, it wouldn't surprise me if half my class just happened to go and see them parading about on stage in top hats. It's like they spend their entire lives working out new ways to be embarrassing.

The only good thing about this musical business is that in a few minutes they will both be leaving the house to go to a rehearsal, so I am going to take a break from my labours and go and watch telly until they come back singing about picking a pocket or two or some such nonsense.

LATER

I was settled in front of the telly when Rachel came in and said, 'Aren't you meant to be studying?' in her most irritating big sister voice.

'Aren't you?' I said.

She glared at me. 'Mum and Dad told me to keep an eye on you, so that's what I'm doing.'

'Well, now you've seen me,' I said. 'Oh, come on, Rachel, I'm allowed to take breaks.'

Rachel sighed and stopped looking so grown up.

'I suppose so,' she said. 'Shove over.'

And then she slumped down next to me on the couch, and we spent a very relaxing hour watching *Laurel Canyon* until we heard the car in the drive.

'Quick, turn it off!' said Rachel, and we both sprang off the couch and ran into the kitchen where Rachel quickly put the kettle on.

'Hello, girls,' said Mum when she came in. 'What are you up to? Haven't you been studying?'

Honestly! She doesn't trust us at all.

'We're not up to anything,' said Rachel. 'I'm just making me and Bex some nice herbal tea to soothe our nerves after all our hard work.'

'Really,' said Mum. She didn't sound very convinced.

'How was the rehearsal?' I said. Which, if I say so myself, was a brilliant thing to say, because of course they immediately forgot about our studies and started going on about how well everything is going in their ridiculous production, despite the fact that they are not the stars of the show. Even though it's twenty-five years since they were last in a musical and they are the newest members of the musical society, I think they are both secretly disappointed they didn't get huge parts. They're just in the chorus, though Dad is also understudying the Beadle, the man who runs the workhouse where poor little Oliver lives. Mum isn't even understudying anyone, but, as I pointed out to her, there aren't really very many parts in *Oliver!* for older ladies. She didn't seem very comforted by this, though.

Anyway, they blathered about the musical for a while and

got so enthusiastic that they forgot to lecture me and Rachel about studying. They even let us watch some telly, as though we were just normal girls and not studying slaves. So actually it was quite a nice evening in the end.

WEDNESDAY ❧

Oh dear. I had forgotten that in a moment of what I can only describe as insanity I told Mrs Harrington that my mum was going to name a character in her next book after her. I just did it out of guilt because Mrs Harrington had really wanted to meet Mum, and I'd managed to arrange it so their paths didn't cross, so I told Mrs Harrington a total lie to cheer her up. I know it was stupid but it somehow seemed like a good idea at the time. Like I said, it was a moment of insanity.

Anyway, I hoped she'd forgotten about it because she hasn't mentioned it in weeks, but of course she hasn't, as she proved when she pounced on me today. Luckily she waited until our English class was over and we were all going off to lunch so none of my classmates witnessed it all.

'Now, Rebecca,' she said. 'I know it's a bit cheeky, but I was wondering if you know what sort of character your mammy has named after me in her new book? Gerard and I are so excited. He thinks it'll probably be a teacher, like me, but I have a feeling it's going to be a nurse. Or the heroine's mother.'

Good lord. She has been thinking about this far too much. As has Gerard, apparently. Gerard is her husband who is just as much of a crazed fan of my mother as his wife. Although in fairness you'd never guess if you met him, he seems quite normal.

I managed to get out of it by saying, 'Oh, Mum never tells us details about her books until they're finished,' which was another total lie. But I know I'm only putting off the terrible day when she eventually picks up my mum's new book and realises there's no Mrs Harrington in it. Or whatever her first name is. She did tell me at one stage, 'so you can tell your mammy', but I've forgotten. Was it Eileen? I have a feeling it was Eileen.

Anyway, I told Cass and Alice at lunch, but they weren't as sympathetic as I'd hoped.

'Why on earth did you say it in the first place?' said Cass. 'It's not as if she even suggested your mum put her in a book! It was all your idea!'

'I don't know why!' I said miserably. 'I just felt guilty because she was so disappointed when my mum didn't turn up that night. Although I don't know why I felt bad for her, considering how much she's tormented me all year going on about how she loves my "mammy's lovely books".' (I did what I think was quite a good impression of Mrs Harrington for that last bit.)

'Maybe you could persuade your mum to actually put Mrs Harrington into the book?' suggested Alice.

'But then I'd have to tell Mum that I lied to Mrs Harrington,' I said. 'She won't be very happy if she thinks I've been going around telling people they can be in the next Rosie Carberry book.'

'Don't worry, you'll figure something out,' said Cass cheerfully, which was a bit callous, I thought. She could have shown a bit more concern for my plight. 'Now, let's talk about a bigger issue – the future of Hey Dollface. We need to sort out our summer plans. Like regular practices.'

'I wish we could have regular practices,' said Alice sadly. 'If only I lived nearer town.'

We practise out in Alice's place, because there are all these barns and old stables and things next to the house. The thing is, the only reason they have all that space is because they live in the middle of the countryside near Kinsealy, and it's hard for me and Cass to get out there. There's a bus that comes about once every two weeks (well, that's what it feels like if you miss it), and even if you get it, the bus stop is about twenty minutes' walk from Alice's house. So basically we have to rely on getting lifts, which doesn't suit any of our parents, and will suit them even less once the holidays start and we want to go out there during the week when they're all at work.

Of course, my mum works at home, so technically she could easily take a break and give me and Cass a lift, but she gets very annoyed if you suggest that working from home is in any way different from working in an office. Over the Easter holidays I tried to get her to take us out to Kinsealy, and she acted like I'd interrupted her while she was in the middle of doing some brain surgery.

'I'm at work, Rebecca!' she said when I knocked on the door of her study. 'Would you go in to your dad if he was at work giving a lecture and ask him for a lift?'

I was just about to say, 'Well, Dad wouldn't be wearing pyjama bottoms at work and you are.' But I didn't because I knew it would increase her wrath.

Anyway, we are trying to think of ways to get around the lift/bus issue but it's not looking good.

'Maybe we could get a rehearsal space somewhere in town?' said Cass. 'Liz says that her big sister's band rent a place on Parnell Square. It's a bit ramshackle, and the loo doesn't work very well, but it's okay.' Liz is in a band called Bad Monkey who we met at the Battle of the Bands, and she and Cass have become good friends.

'But that costs money,' I said. 'And isn't Liz's sister in college? I mean, I don't think our parents would give us the cash to just go to some manky old studio somewhere.'

'You're probably right,' admitted Cass. 'Oh well. We'll just have to get really good at timing the buses.'

She's right, we can manage it. It's not the end of the world if we have to keep on practising at Alice's place. It's just that it would be good to be able to practise more often. Imagine if we could practise every day! We'd be, like, professional quality musicians by the end of the summer.

THURSDAY ◎

I am studying again! Well, obviously I'm not, I'm writing this, but I'm meant to be studying. The problem is that I have now read so much about the Reformation my eyes are starting to glaze over, so I need to take a break from my academic labours. But I will still be technically working, because I'm going to come up with a list of what we need to do to make Hey Dollface the best band in Dublin.

1. Practise loads.

We have been practising as much as possible recently, despite the difficulties of getting out to Alice's place, because we had to make up for lost time. It's now three months since Alice fell off a chair at Vanessa's ridiculous birthday party and fractured her wrist. Which of course meant she couldn't play the guitar and the band had to go on hiatus for ages and ages.

Of course, after Alice fractured her wrist, we had the whole school musical thing to occupy us, but even taking part in the greatest production of *Mary Poppins* ever didn't make up for the fact that we were missing out on weeks and weeks of practising. A few months ago I thought we'd be, like, total band experts by summer. But Cass still sometimes gets the rhythms wrong in her keyboard basslines, and I still have moments when I sort of forget how to play the drums at all.

Weirdly, Alice, the one who was actually physically unable to play her instrument for weeks and weeks, makes fewer mistakes than either of us. Maybe she was just, like, saving her musical strength during all those weeks in a cast. Anyway, she is very devoted to the Hey Dollface cause and has made lots of time to practise since the cast came off, which is particularly good because she is the only one of us with a boyfriend and she doesn't get to see him during the week. There are some people who would ditch their old friends at the weekends when a new love came along, but not Alice. She is a good friend AND a good bandmate. Of course, her boyfriend, Richard, aka Bike Boy, understands because he is in a band too. They respect each other's work.

Sometimes I sort of wish I had a boyfriend too, but, actually, it is quite peaceful not having a distracting boy to think about. For ages I was thinking of lovely Paperboy, then he moved to Canada, and I was thinking about him in a sad way, and then I was thinking about John Kowalski from the musical, and then I realised that he was a selfish smelly fool and not worth thinking about at all. And since then there have been no boys at all. I was worried it might be a bit boring without somebody to think about and be excited about seeing. But actually it is a relief. I can think about lots of other things, like books, and the story I've started writing, and how we're going to play loads of gigs this summer and become the greatest band ever. Well, you never know. As Alice said, 'We've got to have ambition.'

Which brings me on to number two on our list.

2. Play gigs. Preferably loads of them.

To be honest, I thought we'd have played more gigs by now, because when we finished the musical we were sure we were going to put on a show with Bad Monkey. But by the time Alice's wrist was better it was so near the summer tests that none of us had time to organise a gig (or, rather, our evil parents won't let us) so it somehow hasn't happened yet. The problem is that, as we are all under eighteen, we have to arrange an afternoon gig, and that is easier said than done. I think it's very unfair that we can't play gigs in the evening. Mum explained that venues don't want to host under-eighteens nights because that means they have to close the bar and they generally make most of their profits selling booze, but I think they should be noble and sacrifice a few euro for the sake of the future of music.

But we're going to manage to play a gig somehow. Whenever I remember the (very short) bit of the Battle of the Bands when it all seemed to come together and the crowd were all cheering and dancing, I feel all tingly and sparkling inside. It made all the annoying practising bits when I couldn't play the drums properly worthwhile.

And, well, that's it. I suppose it's not really much of a list if there are only two things on it. But anyway, it's a mission statement: practise lots, and play gigs. And maybe get, like, a manager who could sort all that out for us. Although I don't think that's very likely.

Right, back to my studies again. I know that in a few weeks I'll be able to relax in the evenings and read anything I like, but that seems a very long way away right now.

FRIDAY

God, I can't wait until school is over and I don't have to see anyone from that ridiculous place (apart from my actual friends) for three months. Today Miss Kelly started grilling us on where we were going on holidays.

'I hope none of you are going to be getting in an aeroplane, girls,' she said sternly. 'The more people fly, the quicker all the oil runs out.'

'Where are you going on holiday, Miss Kelly?' said Cass, who has always been very good at distracting teachers. It is one of her main talents. She has often wondered if she could use this skill in some sort of career.

'I'm cycling to the south of France with a group of friends,' said Miss Kelly, proudly. 'One hundred per cent pedal powered!'

We all stared at her.

'But, um, what about the sea bit?' said Cass.

'Ah, we have to resort to a ferry from Rosslare to Cherbourg,' admitted Miss Kelly. 'But that's much less environmentally damaging than getting a plane. And if I didn't get ferries, I'd never be able to leave the country. I see it as my duty as a geographer to see the world.'

Which is fair enough, I suppose. But still, I think it's a bit much of Miss Kelly to be giving out to us about our holiday destinations as well as giving us horrible geography exams.

I suppose it wasn't all bad today, though. My parents deigned to let me go over to Cass's house after school. I'm still jealous of her bedroom; it's so much cooler than mine. I am going to have to make my parents let me do mine up this summer, it's ridiculous having such a babyish room when I'm practically fifteen. I can even do it myself. How hard can it be to paint over some wallpaper? All I need is some paint and a ladder. And a brush, obviously.

Anyway, Cass and I lay on her bed and ate some Pringles and had deep conversations about LIFE and love.

'You haven't heard anything from you-know-who, have you?' said Cass.

'Which you-know-who?' I said. Because I genuinely didn't know.

'John,' said Cass.

'Oh, him,' I said crossly. Not that I was cross at Cass. Just at the thought of John. 'No, I'd have told you if I had. I thought I saw him on Griffith Avenue the other day but it was someone else.'

'Someone less of a stinker, probably,' said Cass. 'And what about ...'

I knew she meant Paperboy. It doesn't hurt so much thinking about him anymore, not like after he went to Canada and I was a hollow shell of a girl. I know he isn't coming back, and I know we're not getting back together, and I don't really mind.

But there is a part of me that feels all sad whenever I think about him. Every so often I hear a song that reminds me of when we were going out or even of the time before that when I really fancied him and got all excited whenever he called to our house to collect the money for the papers. And it's like something washes right over me and I'm back there for a second. But then I have to go back to the boring old present day. I didn't want to go on about this too much to Cass. I do remember the days when I kept moping about Paperboy's disappearance, and it started to drive my friends mad because I didn't really pay attention to anything either of them said. So I told her that I'd heard from Paperboy last week and he was fine.

'But I still feel weird when I get a mail or a message from him,' I said. 'And whenever anything really reminds me of him I feel a bit sad. And I really, really don't want to know if he's going out with someone else. Does that mean I'm still moping?'

'I don't think so,' said Cass. 'I think it would be weird if you'd, like, totally forgotten about him. And I think maybe you always feel a bit odd when you hear someone you used to go out with is going out with someone else. It doesn't mean you're still madly in love with him or pining after him or anything like that. It's just normal.'

Cass may not be personally experienced in the ways of love, but she is certainly full of wisdom. Sometimes, anyway. And then we stopped talking about love and talked about ways we could earn money over the holidays in order to pay for a practice space. Cass suggested we could make sweets like fudge and sell them at farmers' markets.

'There's one in Saint Anne's Park in Raheny on Saturdays,' she said. 'We could take our wares there and sell them among the farmers.'

This seemed like a very good idea.

'Ooh, yes,' I said. 'And we'd stand out because we'd be the youngest people there, and everyone would be really impressed. And we could call our sweet company Hey Dollface and sell the sweets at our gigs!'

'Yes!' said Cass. 'And the whole thing would hardly cost anything. I mean, I bet we could get little bags or boxes in a supermarket for a euro or two. And then the ingredients wouldn't cost very much. What do you need to make fudge?'

'Um ... I'm not sure,' I said. 'Sugar, probably.'

'Vanilla essence,' said Cass knowledgeably. 'And ... um ... butter? Maybe eggs?'

And then we realised that neither of us have ever made fudge before. Or any sweets. In fact, the only sugary foodstuff I've ever made was a slightly soggy lemon drizzle cake over the Christmas holidays. But, as I told Cass, it was quite delicious even if it was soggy (and despite the fact I got slightly nervous whenever I turned on the electric hand mixer in case I lost control of it and it sliced my fingers off, even though Mum kept saying that wasn't going to happen).

'Can we actually sell soggy cake, though?' said Cass. 'Or whatever the fudge equivalent of soggy cake is?'

'Well, I bet we'd get the hang of it with a little bit of practice,' I said. I mean, how hard could it be?

LATER

I mentioned my and Cass's plans to become artisan farmers' market sweet makers to my mother, and she LAUGHED. She does nothing but crush my dreams.

'I'm sorry, love,' she said when she'd stopped laughing. 'It's just that I think you might need a bit more practice before you can sell sweets at that market. And possibly some sort of food production licence.'

Honestly, the way she goes on about how much she and Dad spend on me and Rachel, you'd think she'd welcome my plans to earn my own money, but no! Talent and initiative are not encouraged in this family.

SUNDAY ☼

My father has abandoned us! But only for a few days. He has gone off to a conference in Oxford. Dad is an academic, which in his case means he is basically a fancy history teacher, and every so often he goes off to England or New Jersey or Istanbul for conferences where he meets lots of other history teachers, and they all stand around talking about Early Modern European History, which is Dad's supposed 'speciality'. And what they call Early Modern European History isn't very modern at all. It's, like, six hundred years ago, which makes no sense. But

I shouldn't expect something to make sense if my dad, a man who once played the part of a dancing pirate on stage while wearing gold harem pants, has anything to do with it.

He's gone to some college in Oxford called Shrewsbury which used to be an all-female college. As I am in an all-girls school and never get to meet any boys ever I can't imagine anyone wanting to go to an all-girls college afterwards (unless they liked girls, obviously), but when I said this to my mum she said that women's colleges had a fine tradition in educating girls and that actually girls sometimes do better when there are no boys around, which is fair enough. But I still think I would like to go to a college with boys in it. I know I said I quite like not having a distracting boy in my life right now, but I have to admit that sometimes I worry that I'll never go out with anyone ever again. And the chances of that happening would be higher if I went straight from an all-girls school to an all-girls college.

Anyway, Dad is going to spend a few days at Shrewsbury listening to all his history mates blathering on about wars and other such nonsense. He is flying into London, and Rachel started giving him a list of things to get her in the duty free, including a replacement for the amazing Chanel lipstick that suits everyone and which I am fond of borrowing myself without telling her (which is possibly why it's run out and she needs a new one).

'And who, pray tell, will be paying for all this?' he said.

'Early birthday present,' said Rachel hopefully.

'No,' said Dad. But he took the list anyway so I bet he'll end up getting her one thing. I hope it's the lipstick, for selfish reasons. He turned to me. 'Do you want anything from England, Bex?'

Perhaps he is not so bad after all. Right now I can't help thinking he is being nicer than my dream-crushing mother.

But, of course, as soon as he made this kindly offer I couldn't think of anything I wanted so I said I'd text him. I need to take advantage of this unusual generosity so I will have to have a think.

MONDAY ☀

I don't believe it. I think Vanessa and Karen might have solved our band issues! Apart from finding us a manager, obviously. But the practising and the gigging and stuff. In fact, they might have solved our entire summer. In theory I feel I should thank them but I can't bring myself to do it.

It happened during the morning break today. We were sitting around in our classroom talking about our plans for the summer, which in most people's cases were non-existent, apart from Emma who's going to the Gaeltacht with her best friend from home. Vanessa was sitting around the next desk with what I am appalled to say is now her gang – her old sidekick Caroline, of course, and now Karen 'Bitchface' Rodgers, my nemesis. She and Vanessa have become all chummy since they both got starring roles in the musical. Luckily, Caroline and Karen's friend Alison have sort of teamed up. Both of them are nicer than Karen and Vanessa and, in fact, would be completely fine if they just stopped hanging around with them. So we hoped that they would break away completely and form a gang of their own. But sadly that hasn't happened yet, and the four of them are hanging around together.

ANYWAY. Emma was talking about going to the Gaeltacht, and Ellie said, 'I wish you could go to, like, summer art college instead of Irish college.' And then Vanessa, who never minds interrupting other people's conversations (although of course I am glad she did in this case), said, 'God, haven't you heard of the North Dublin Arts Camp?'

And we all stared at her in surprise, because we hadn't.

'What's that?' said Ellie.

'I can't believe you don't know about it,' said Vanessa, smugly. 'I've had my place in the drama group booked for weeks. So has Karen.' And both of them looked so pleased with themselves I thought I was going to get sick.

'But what is it?' said Cass, through what I could tell were gritted teeth.

'It's, like, a summer school for, like, teenage actors and artists and musicians and stuff,' said Vanessa. She said it was in the big college down the road, and that it started in June. 'You don't stay overnight, but you go in every day and have workshops and put on, like, shows and exhibitions.'

'Me and Bernard – that's my boyfriend – are going to get to act together at last,' said Karen. 'He's doing the acting school too.'

I felt as if a light bulb had lit up over my head. Not at the thought of Karen's stupid boyfriend Bernard – who she met when he was employed to play a fairy-tale prince at Vanessa's party and who we've all heard enough about over the last few months – but at the words 'musicians' and 'shows'.

'So what sort of musicians can do it?' I said. 'Like, classical musicians?'

'Oh, I don't know,' said Karen loftily. 'I only care about the theatre.'

But then Vanessa said, 'God, Karen, you don't pay attention to anything'. Which was a bit rich, coming from her. I don't think she's ever consciously listened to anyone else in her life. 'They're doing some sort of thing for, like, bands,' she continued. 'They're calling it a rock school. They're going to put on, like, little gigs and stuff.'

Cass and Alice and I looked at each other. I knew we were all thinking the same thing. We had a half day today (hurrah) because the teachers were having some sort of meeting (probably plotting all the horrible tests they're going to give us), so Alice was going round to Cass's house to wait for her lift. I went there too so we could all look up the camp online. And it was true, there was a rock school! Where proper grown-up bands would come in and, like, coach you! And you got to learn how to record and put on shows and everything! It was like the answer to our prayers.

'We must go to this!' said Cass. 'I just hope it's not too late.'

'Let's all ring our parents and see if they'll let us go,' said

Alice, sensibly. 'And then we can book our place right now.'

So that's what we did. Luckily, I had enough credit on my phone (for once). I was sure that Mum would make a fuss, as she normally does everything she can to stand in the way of my happiness, but to my surprise she didn't.

'Well, that does sound like a good idea,' she said. 'It's quite good value too. And it'll save me and Brenda giving you and Cass lifts. I'll have to check with your dad, though.'

'Thank you, thank you, thank you!' I said. 'You're the best mother in the world!' Which is not what I think most of the time, but I did mean it when I said it. Anyway, she rang Dad in Oxford, and, luckily, he wasn't listening to people blathering on about history at the time and could answer his phone. Then she rang me straight back.

'Your dad says yes,' she said. 'Now don't say we never do anything for you.'

I ran into Cass's kitchen, and her parents and Alice's parents had all said yes too (though Cass's mum said that if she did badly in her summer tests she was still going to have to go to a maths school. I don't think this will happen, though, as Cass has actually been studying quite hard and, really, she's pretty good at maths when she actually tries).

'Now we just have to hope there are spaces left,' said Cass. And she took a deep breath and tapped the number of the Arts Camp office into the phone. 'Go out of the room!' she hissed at me and Alice. 'I'll get nervous talking to the camp people if you're watching.'

So we went out into the hall. A minute later we could hear Cass going, 'I'm ringing to see if there are any more places for bands on the North Dublin Arts Camp' and 'Yes' and 'No' and 'Okay' and 'Thanks very much'.

'This could be good or bad,' said Alice nervously. But then Cass came out, and she was beaming.

'There are a few places left!' she said. 'Apparently they only added the band bit of the camp at the last minute so it hasn't been as well publicised as the art and drama things. So I've booked us in, and our parents have to ring and pay by next week.'

'A few places left!' said Alice. 'Maybe Richard and the Wicked Ways would like to do it too!' She wanted to ring him straight away, but then she remembered that he didn't have a half day.

'Maybe Bad Monkey could do it too?' I said.

'Nah,' said Cass, looking a bit disappointed. 'Liz and Katie are going to be in Irish college for the first two weeks of it.' But she cheered up when we started looking at more details about the course on the website.

'Just think,' she said. 'This is just what we need. A place to practise. Mentors to teach us the ways of rock!'

It is all very exciting. I couldn't stay for too long because I was meant to be coming straight home after school and Mum was making dinner early, but Alice texted me later to say that Richard and the Wicked Ways had managed to get a place too. It's a pity about Bad Monkey not being able to do it, though. Liz is really nice and funny. She and Cass see each other a lot, and it is proof of how much I like her that I don't really feel jealous, even though Cass has found a new friend. Well, I only sometimes feel a bit jealous. In fact, we've all made friends this year. Like Jane, who we met at Vanessa's terrible party and who ended up saving the day at our musical.

Ooh. Maybe she'd like to do the arts camp too? She could do the drama thing, it's not like she's not used to putting up with Vanessa. I will text her now and cross my fingers.

TUESDAY ☾

Oh God. I don't know what's wrong with me. I have got even more stuck in my web of lies to Mrs Harrington. After English today she nabbed me when I was trying to sneak out of the classroom and said, 'So, Rebecca! Did you have a chance to ask your mammy about my character? I don't want to be any hassle, but I'd just love to know!'

And I realised I just had to tell her the truth. Or, okay, not the actual whole truth, which was that I had been lying all the time, but the truth that my mum wasn't going to be putting her in a book. I could tell her that Mum – no, even better, Mum's publisher – had decided she was never going to put any real people in books in case any of them sued her for libel and that she couldn't even make an exception for Mrs Harrington. I took a deep breath.

'There's just one thing ...' I said. This was it. I knew Mrs Harrington would be disappointed, and she might even take it out on me in class (though I had a feeling she wouldn't – she's incredibly annoying but she's not intentionally mean). But I couldn't let this madness go on any longer.

'Yes?' said Mrs Harrington.

And just as I opened my mouth, I realised I couldn't bring myself to tell her. I am a total chicken.

'Um, my mum wanted to make sure she's got the spelling of your name right,' I said. 'How do you spell it again?'

'Just the usual way of spelling Patricia Alexandra,' said Mrs Harrington. 'So, well, P-A-T-R-I-C-I-A and then A-L-E-X-A-N-D-R-A.'

Good heavens. I did not expect her to have a name like that. I thought it would be a lot more ... ordinary. And Irish Mammy-ish.

'Patricia Alexandra?' I said without thinking, in a very surprised voice. 'Really?'

Mrs Harrington looked slightly bemused, as well she might at my suggestion that she didn't know her own name.

'Um, yes,' she said. 'Do you want me to spell it again?'

'Oh, no, that's okay,' I said.

'Well, I can't wait to read all about the fictional Patricia Alexandra Harrington!' said Mrs Harrington happily. 'Let me know how it's going!'

There is only one thing to do. I have to make sure Mum actually puts this character into her next book and names her Patricia Alexandra Harrington, without telling her about my web of lies. I will have to drop lots of helpful hints. The only problem is – well, actually, there are a lot of problems, but one of them is that the last time I tried to suggest plot points to my mother she didn't take them seriously. In fact, she might have even been laughing at me, like the ungrateful woman she is. But I have to give it a try. I can't do anything about it right now as she is off at her *Oliver!* rehearsal. Dad was a bit worried about missing it, though, as Rachel kindly told him, the absence of one chorus member won't really make a huge difference (even if that member of the chorus is understudying the Beadle). She had a point – I mean, I was in the chorus myself in *Mary Poppins*. And even I have to admit that I could have missed one rehearsal without the whole show collapsing. Anyway, Mum can tell him what he's missed.

WEDNESDAY ✿

Even though we're being made to work all the time, I am getting very excited about the summer camp. Ellie is going to do the art course, to hone her dress-designing skills, and Jane has managed to get a place on the drama bit! Her best friend from school, Aoife, is going to visit her aunt in Australia for most of June so she was expecting to be very bored all month and this has cheered her up. Even though Vanessa and Karen will be doing it too.

'I think I might be immune to Vanessa at this stage,' she said on the phone last night. 'After all, we were in that drama class together and then the musical.'

I think she might be a bit too optimistic. After all, I've seen Vanessa almost every day for two years of school and I'm definitely not immune to her yet. But maybe Jane is made of sturdier stuff than I am.

Anyway, Cass printed all the details of the camp so we could look at them together at leisure at school (well, at lunchtime). It looks brilliant. We're going to have these workshops, sometimes just with us and our mentors, sometimes with the other bands, and then we'll be given our own practice rooms and we can work on our own stuff there. And at the end of it we will all play a gig.

'This is going to be the greatest summer ever,' said Alice.

'I wonder if we'll have any time for our sweet-making business?' said Cass.

'We can do it at weekends,' I said.

Alice looked a bit dubious.

'I'm not sure the sweet thing is going to work,' she said. 'I mean, it's a great idea, but don't you need a bit more experience?'

Honestly! She's as bad as my mother.

'We're going to get some experience!' said Cass.

'Exactly!' I said. 'Come over to my house and we can give it a try.'

Alice can't go on Saturday because she's meeting Richard. I will have to beg my parents (or rather my mum, Dad isn't back until Saturday) to let me leave my studies for a few hours. She'll probably let me, though, because I have been working impressively hard over the last few weeks. I deserve an afternoon off.

THURSDAY ◎

My 'Put Mrs Harrington in a Book' plan has begun. And I think it might actually be working! I am a genius, if I say so myself.

'So, Mum,' I said this evening, while I was peeling potatoes like the domestic servant I am (my parents would prefer it if I did nothing but study and peel vegetables. Though at least today as Dad is still away there were slightly fewer vegetables to peel than usual). 'How's the new grown-up book coming along?'

Mum is writing a new book for adults because she finished her second terrible book about a girl my age a few months ago. At least, I assume it's terrible. I haven't read it yet, but the last one was awful, AND it basically ruined my life for a while so I'm not looking forward to the second one, even though Mum says she's learned her lesson and is going to make sure everyone knows that Ruthie Reilly in the book has nothing to do with either of the author's children.

Anyway, Mum is taking a break from writing about irritating teenagers (thank GOD) and is returning to her usual sort of book about kindly mammies and middle-aged ladies finding love and setting up cafés in villages and stuff. Surely, I thought, there must be room for a Patricia Alexandra Harrington figure in there somewhere.

'Oh, it's early days, but it's going okay,' said Mum. She looked quite pleased to see me taking an interest in her books again. She used to like telling us about the plots and letting us know how the writing was coming along, but after Rachel and I got so annoyed about Ruthie last year she has kept quite quiet about it. All I knew was that she'd started another book and that it was for grown-ups.

'Do you know what it's about yet?' I said.

'Yes, more or less,' said Mum. 'Careful with that potato peeler!'

'I am being careful,' I said. 'So what's it about? There are no fourteen-year-olds in it, are there? Or even fifteen-year-olds?'

Mum laughed. 'No,' she said. 'The only children in it are under ten. There is absolutely no chance anyone will mistake you for any of them.'

Well, I suppose that's something, at least. Anyway, it turns out the new book is about a woman who moves to a little village (I have said this before, but I have no idea why my mother writes about little villages all the time, considering she's from Phibsboro and has lived in north Dublin for her entire life) and opens a bakery and falls in love with a local farmer who supplies the bakery with eggs. It sounds dreadful, but all her books do, to be honest, and lots of people really do love them (though probably not as much as Mrs Harrington and Gerard do).

'Does this woman have a name?' I said hopefully.

'Yes,' said Mum. 'Lily Fitzsimons. It's perfect for her.'

Damn.

'So are there any other main characters?' I said. Surely there was someone who could be called Patricia Alexandra Harrington?

'Well, there's the farmer's sister who tries to get them together,' said Mum. 'And I think I'm going to put in a local teacher whose kids go to the bakery after school ...'

That was it! Or rather, her. How absolutely perfect.

'What's she called?' I said.

'She doesn't have a name yet,' said Mum. 'She's just a vague sort of character at the moment.'

'What about ...' I pretended to think about it for a moment. 'Patricia Alexandra Harrington?'

Mum laughed. 'Wow, you're very helpful all of a sudden! What brought this on?'

'I'm just grateful you're not writing another book about stupid Ruthie,' I said.

'Hmmm,' said Mum. 'Actually, that's not a bad name. It might work.' She smiled. 'I'll thank you in the acknowledgements if I go with it!'

I didn't want to push it, but I think my scheme might have worked. I'm actually a bit surprised, to be honest. Surely it can't be as easy as this? Maybe it can.

FRIDAY ☺

I feel a bit weird. Guess who I saw on my way home from school today?

John Kowalski.

It's been ages and ages since I've seen him – not since we had our huge fight the day of the musical. So it took me by surprise. It was on Griffith Avenue, of course. I'd just said goodbye to Cass and was about to cross the road and go up Gracepark Road when I glanced around, and there he was, walking along with a strange girl. When I say strange, I mean that she was a stranger to me, not that she had, like, two heads or was wearing fake antlers, or anything. She looked totally normal. Anyway, he looked pretty surprised to see me too, but only for a second, and then his face returned to its usual haughty expression, and he said, 'Oh, hello Rafferty.'

I had been going to walk on, but he stopped. And I felt it

was too rude to just march past so I stopped too. Really I am too polite for my own good sometimes.

'Hi John,' I said. I waited for him to introduce the girl, but he didn't so I looked at her and said, 'Hi, I'm Rebecca.'

She looked a bit shy and nervous and said, 'Um, I'm Aoife.'

I assume she is his new girlfriend because she was gazing at him in a rather adoring way. I noticed they weren't holding hands, but then I remembered John's stupid rule about not showing any sort of human affection in public. And how he didn't want to call me his girlfriend because he hated being 'tied down with labels'. I hope for her sake that Aoife doesn't mind all that nonsense because I certainly did.

'So, Rafferty,' said John, and I have to admit that when he looked at me in that sort of amused, sort of arrogant way and called me by my surname I did feel a bit funny for a minute. It reminded me how I really did like him for a while back then, despite everything. And by everything I mean him being a selfish, snobby, cigarette-smelling fool. 'What are you up to these days? I hope you're not frittering away your time with nonsense.'

And now I remembered why I broke up with him.

'No,' I said. 'I'm getting ready for an amazing summer

49

music camp. Me and Cass and Alice are doing it with the band. Richard's doing it too. It's going to be brilliant.'

John looked slightly taken aback for a minute.

'Oh, right,' he said. Then he said, 'I'll be concentrating on my writing, of course. Maybe doing a bit of acting. Expanding my creative horizons.'

'What about you?' I said to Aoife. She looked taken aback too.

'Oh,' she said. 'I think I'll be writing too. John's been really encouraging my poetry. He thinks if I work hard I could be a really serious writer.'

'Yes,' said John. 'Aoife's really getting to understand great literature. Neither of us have any time for frivolous fluff.'

Good grief. He hasn't changed a bit. Well, all I can say is that I hope Aoife is actually writing stuff she likes, and that if she isn't she'll see the light and not let John show off and boss her about all the time, like he tried to do with me. I really did have a narrow escape.

But I didn't say this to Aoife, of course. I just said, 'Oh, cool. Anyway, I'd better go ...'

'See you around, Rafferty,' said John in a grand voice. Aoife gave me a shy sort of half-wave, and they were off down the other end of Gracepark Road. And that was that. I walked home feeling very odd. Not in a 'Oh, I wish I was still going out with him' way, because I certainly do not. In fact, I'm relieved that I'm not still going out with him, because he is terrible. I suppose Cass is right. Maybe you do feel funny about your exes for ages afterwards. Even if you would rather get sick than ever go out with them again.

Dad is coming home tomorrow. I hate to admit it but I have quite missed him. I've texted him asking him to get me one of those lovely lipsticks like Rachel's one for my very own.

SATURDAY ☺

Today Cass and I began our new lives as amazing sweet-makers. It was a bit of a rocky start, of course, but I'm sure we'll get better soon. We weren't helped by my mother acting like we were eight years old. She kept hovering over us and going on about how boiling sugar was really dangerous and that we weren't to touch it – as if we would, we're not mad. Eventually I had to tell her that if she actually wanted us to have a hideous accident the best way to make this happen was to stand right next to us and keep distracting us by going on about the dangers of cookery. So she went to the other end of the kitchen and looked at us nervously.

Of course, she needn't have worried. We were fine. The trickiest bit was after the fudge had boiled and we had to stir it really hard for about ten minutes. It turns out that, even with all my drumming and Cass's keyboard playing, we have very feeble wrists. And stirring fudge is really hard work. Eventually we had to give in and ask my mum if she'd take a turn, but she was going out to collect my dad from the airport so she couldn't.

'I was only waiting until you'd got past the dangerous boiling sugar stage,' she said. 'I'm running late already. Your dad's flight is due in a few minutes.'

So we had to keep beating it ourselves.

'I think my wrist is going to fall off,' I said after we'd had a few turns each.

'Well, if Alice was here there'd be three of us and it would be easier,' said Cass, taking the wooden spoon. 'We could take shorter turns.' She stirred and stirred until she was red in the face. Then she dropped the spoon in the bowl, exhausted.

'Has it been ten minutes yet?' she said.

I looked at my watch.

'More or less,' I said.

So we left it to set, as the instructions advised.

'You know,' said Cass, as we drank some refreshing lemonade while the fudge did its thing, 'if this all works out, we might even get our own cookery show on telly. Teenage cooks! Who are also in a band! I think it could work.'

'Ooh, and we could play a song in each episode,' I said. 'That could be our gimmick.'

'What are you blathering on about?' said Rachel, wandering into the kitchen.

'Our plans to be celebrity-cooks-slash-rock-goddesses,' said Cass.

Rachel laughed in a not very supportive way.

'Ha! Well, let me know how that works out for you,' she said, and strolled out again.

'Huh,' I said. 'What does she know?'

'Yeah, she'll be sorry when we're incredibly famous and she's begging to be allowed on our show,' said Cass. 'Is the fudge set yet?'

But it wasn't, so Cass had the excellent idea of designing some labels for the boxes in which we will sell our wares. Cass wants to design theatre sets, and she's pretty good at designing other things too. Of course, she consulted with me, and after a while she came up with a cool little logo with the words Hey Dollface written in two different types of lettering.

'I bet we'll be the only band who sell home-made sweets at their gigs,' she said happily. And then it was finally time to taste our creation. We carefully cut it into squares and took one each.

'Well, it's not horrible,' said Cass after a long pause.

'It's not quite the same as fudge from a shop,' I said. 'But then, that's because it's home-made and fresh and made from simple ingredients.'

'Is it meant to taste so ... gritty? And crumbly?' said Cass.

'Maybe that's what real genuine fudge tastes like,' I said doubtfully.

That was when Rachel came in.

'Oh, is it ready then?' she said, and before we could answer she just grabbed some fudge from the baking tray and shoved a piece into her greedy gob.

'Hmmm,' she said, when she'd swallowed it.

'Hmmm what?' I said. 'Hmmm, that's the most delicious authentic home-made fudge I've ever eaten?'

'More like hmmm, I can't believe you think you could

actually sell this,' said Rachel. 'You'd get arrested.' We asked her what was so wrong with it, but she just kept saying it tasted 'funny'. We were still discussing it when my parents came back.

'I'm home!' said Dad cheerfully. 'What's that nice smell?'

I looked triumphantly at Rachel.

'It's lovely fudge which Cass and I have made as a home-coming gift for you,' I said, not entirely truthfully.

'Aw, thanks, girls!' said Dad and took a piece. 'Mmmm!' He chewed it thoughtfully and then swallowed. 'Um, it's very good for a first try. But maybe the next batch could be a bit more ... I dunno. Fudgy?'

I give up. It's no use trying to impress my family. They don't know anything about food. Anyway, soon after Dad arrived, Cass had to go home and study, and I had to stay here and study (which is what I'm meant to be doing now), but we are going to try making more fudge as soon as either of our parents will let us take over the kitchen. Which, sadly, probably won't be until these stupid summer tests are over.

It's quite nice to have Dad back, though. He got me the lipstick, too.

MONDAY ☀

I don't believe it. That little Mulligan kid who lives across the road from us is back to her old tricks. And by her old tricks I mean staring at me from her bedroom window when I'm trying to work in my own room and making hideous faces at me. She hasn't done it for a while, and I thought she'd got sick of it at last, but no! This evening I was just sitting there minding my own business and trying to study boring old algebra when I glanced up and saw her staring in at me from across the road. And as soon as she saw me looking at her, she started gyrating from the left side of the window to the right and then back again, staring at me the entire time. I have to admit it was kind of mesmerising for a minute, but then I made a face at her (childish I know, but I was DRIVEN to it) and pulled across the curtain. So now I am writing in the dark even though it's a lovely sunny evening. What a horrible little freak she is.

TUESDAY ☾

Oh my God. My plan to get Mum to put Mrs Harrington

in a book has worked, but not in a good way! What have I done? Today after English Mrs Harrington asked me how the fictional Patricia Alexandra Harrington was coming along, which reminded me that I'd better nudge Mum. So when I came home from school, and Rachel was supposedly studying (but really on the phone to Tom, the boyfriend), I said, very casually, 'So, did you name a character Patricia Alexandra Harrington like I suggested, then?'

Mum looked a bit surprised that I was asking about her work unprovoked, but also quite pleased.

'I actually did!' she said. 'So thanks for that.'

I couldn't believe it.

'Seriously?' I said. 'That's brilliant!'

Mum laughed. 'You're not usually so enthusiastic about inspiring my books!' she said.

'Well, this is different,' I said. 'The last time I didn't realise I was doing any inspiring. And I didn't want to be inspiring anyway. This time it was my idea.'

'Fair enough,' said Mum. 'Anyway, thanks.'

'So, what's she like?' I said. 'The Patricia Alexandra Harrington in the book?'

'Well, she's the teacher in the local school,' said Mum. 'And the kids from her school come into the bakery where the heroine works.'

'Yeah, you told me about that before,' I said. 'So what sort of a person is she? Is she, I dunno, funny? Does she become the heroine's best friend?'

'Oh no, quite the opposite,' said Mum. 'She's the baddie! Well, sort of the baddie.'

'What?' I said.

'Yeah, she doesn't want her students going into the shop at lunch because she thinks they're eating too many cakes and buns so she starts a campaign against Lily, the heroine, and tries to destroy the business,' said Mum. 'It's turned into a good little subplot – it's added another problem for Lily to overcome.'

This was terrible. This was not what I wanted at all. What will Mrs Harrington think when she reads the book and sees that the baddie is named after her? She'll be horrified. She might even think it was all some sort of mean joke! I mean, I know she's really annoying and everything, but she's just annoying, she's not actually evil. I wish she wasn't my English teacher, but I don't actually want to wreak a terrible revenge on her. Also, if she thinks I've been encouraging my mother to do something so nasty, English classes will be even worse than they already are.

'Are you sure about this?' I said. 'Maybe she could be nice instead and encourage all the kids to eat cakes in, you know, moderation.'

'Thanks, Bex,' said Mum. 'But I don't think that would be a very interesting plot line, unlike having a villain who's trying to destroy the heroine's business.'

'I think it'd be very interesting!' I said. I thought for a moment. 'And it would give a positive message about healthy eating,' I added in a very saintly voice.

'Who's writing this book, you or me?' laughed Mum. 'I do appreciate your input, love, but I'd rather have Patricia Alexandra Harrington as a villain, thanks.'

I told her I thought she was making a terrible mistake, but she wasn't convinced. Oh God. I'll just have to keep working on her and try and change her mind.

WEDNESDAY ✿

Everyone is very excited about the summer camp. Ellie is

particularly relieved because it has given her an excuse not to go to the summer programme her mother was suggesting. Ellie's mum is a mystical hippie type, and she wanted Ellie to go to some sort of Inner Goddess camp in Leitrim.

'It would be three weeks of writing poems about periods,' said Ellie. 'And drawing pictures of our inner goddess.' She shuddered.

But in fairness to Ellie's mother, she wasn't going to force Ellie to go to Inner Goddess Camp against her will, especially now there's another summer school she actually wants to attend. Ellie is hoping to hone her art skills and further her dream of being a costume designer. Her mother actually approves of this, because she herself is always weaving fabric to make her own cloaks and other such dramatic garments. So it's all worked out quite well.

Of course, Karen and Vanessa are going on about the camp too. They spent most of lunchtime telling poor old Caroline and Alison about various acting techniques which they plan to learn. (I know this because they were speaking so loudly everyone in the entire classroom could hear them whether we wanted to or not. Which I certainly didn't.) It was both boring and irritating, which is the worst of all combinations.

'I suppose we shouldn't be too annoyed with them,' said Alice. 'I mean, if it wasn't for them we wouldn't know anything about the camp. We should really be thankful to them.'

Just then we heard Vanessa say, very loudly, 'I bet there'll be some agents there. I bet this will be our chance to get discovered. It's only a matter of time.'

'You're so right,' said Karen. 'My boyfriend Bernard was saying the same thing.'

Cass and I looked at Alice.

'Okay,' said Alice. 'Maybe we can just try and ignore them instead.'

But while I'm looking forward to the summer camp, I have more pressing problems right now. Mostly the summer tests, of course, but also the fact that there has been no luck trying to persuade Mum to change Patricia Alexandra Harrington into a goodie. In fact, quite the opposite.

'I don't know why you want me to change her!' said Mum. 'She's working very well as she is. In fact, there was something about that name that somehow made the character come together. She'd been a bit vague before that. But once I had that Patricia Alexandra Harrington name, it was like she turned into a real person.'

Good lord. What have I done?

Anyway, I will keep trying to change her mind, but, in the meantime, I have more to worry about than Mrs Harrington's book stardom. I'm feeling quite nervous about those tests now. I keep telling myself that it's only the second-year summer tests and they don't mean anything, but I can't help it. I keep waking up in the middle of the night, remembering all the things I haven't studied yet – which seems to be nearly everything. This doesn't even make sense, considering my parents have been practically locking me in my room and making me study for weeks, but I'm starting to worry that nothing has gone in. I keep staring at a periodic table, praying for it to stick in my mind before the science test next week but it doesn't seem to be working.

I can't even escape my worries when I'm asleep – last night I had a dreadful dream that I was doing my German exam and John Kowalski appeared and started telling me that he'd just got a part in a big West End production of *King Lear* and that I was wasting time on school. And, actually, turning up at my exam and distracting me by going on about himself is the sort of thing he would definitely do.

LATER

Oh my God. What if Dream-John is right? What if I really am wasting my time on German verbs and scientific elements? Maybe I should drop out of school and concentrate on the band instead. We haven't had a practice for ages what with exams and the various difficulties of getting out to Alice's house. Maybe I should drop out of school and become our full-time manager! Maybe that is where my true talents lie!

LATER

I am not going to drop out of school and become a full-time manager. I think I was just having a wobbler. Actual real-life John was wrong about so many things, so it is very unlikely that my own dream version of him has any wisdom to impart. Also, it would be crazy to drop out of school. Not least because I'm not even fifteen yet, so it would be illegal. And, of course, my parents wouldn't let me. And also, even though I have a lot of faith in Hey Dollface, I think I should probably keep my options open about the whole going-to-college thing.

LATER

Also, all my friends would still be in school. It'd be pretty boring being at home without them. Right, back to the periodic table I go.

THURSDAY ◎

I tried to write some poems this evening when I was taking a break from my hideous studies, but I don't think it's really working. I used to think that my misery over Paperboy moving to Canada fuelled my creative powers, and it seems that I was right! Not that I don't have lots of problems, of course, but they don't seem to be the sort of problems that inspire poetry. I mean, what sort of poem could I write about exams and annoying teachers? Maybe I should try a haiku. They are the easiest sort of poems to write because they are only seventeen syllables long and they don't have to rhyme.

> *Mrs Harrington*
> *Why do you love my mother?*
> *I wish you did not.*

Hmmm, that wasn't that bad, actually, if I say so myself. But still. I just don't feel the old, I dunno, fire. I know I said it was quite relaxing having no boy problems to think about, and it is, but sometimes I can't help wishing something exciting would, you know, just happen. If only to give me something to write about.

Maybe I could write some poems about being a bit bored. But they might be a bit boring.

SATURDAY ☺

Studying. AGAIN. I feel like I can't remember a life when I didn't have to sit in my room staring at books full of stuff I can't remember. I can't wait until I spend an entire day just lazing around doing nothing. Cass has escaped her books for a few hours and has gone into town to meet Liz, but that's only because her parents have gone to a christening and taken her little brother so they can't check up on her. But I am stuck here, trying to avoid looking up at the window because that horrible little Mulligan is back there taunting me. Why hasn't she got anything better to do than sit in her room and annoy her innocent neighbours? I mean, why hasn't she got friends?

LATER

Oh my God, she does have friends! Or at least one friend, who is in her room right now making faces and dancing at me! And now they've turned around and are shaking their bums at me! One annoying child mocking me was bad enough, but two of them is just too much. Surely this is against the law? Maybe I could go to the police.

LATER

Mum says children dancing around in their own rooms isn't against the law. I think it should be, though.

'Just ignore her!' said Mum. 'She's only little.'

Easy for her to say, her study is the other side of the house. I bet if she had to look at some annoying little brats waggling their bums at her when she was trying to write about Lily Fitzsimons, she'd think differently about all this.

SUNDAY ☼

Exams start tomorrow. I am totally panicky. I don't think I have done enough work. I know my parents forced to me to study every night over the last few weeks, but when I look back now I seem to have spent quite a lot of that time writing in my diary. Oh dear.

I have reached a stage where I am basing my studying on what day each exam is on. For example, maths is tomorrow, but history is on Thursday, so I need to concentrate on maths tonight (obviously) and then I will have three more evenings to get various bits of history done. But of course I can't spend all those nights on history because I have other exams too. Like Irish, and German, which are both on Wednesday. Oh God.

Right, I'm going back to work now to try and remember some geometry ... stuff. I can't even remember the words for bits of maths now. Oh dear. I have a feeling I won't be writing in this diary much until it's all over.

WEDNESDAY ✿

I hate exams. I am halfway through exam week, and I have forgotten everything I ever knew. Cass feels the same way, but Alice keeps telling us that we know more than we think.

'You did manage to answer all the questions, didn't you?' she said.

'Yes,' I said. 'But I don't know if I answered them very well.'

'But you actually could answer them,' she said. 'I mean, there was nothing you absolutely couldn't say anything about?'

She is right. But I still don't feel very confident. I am going to go and read some stuff about Martin Luther and hope that some of it sticks in my mind.

SATURDAY ☺

I'm free! I'm free! I'm on my holidays! I can't believe it. I can do anything I like! Anything at all! We had the last tests yester-day (English, not too bad), and then a bunch of us – me, Cass, Alice, Ellie and Emma – all went into town and got delicious burgers and chips. I think we might have drunk too much coke because we were all a bit hyper. And Alice ate too many onion rings and felt quite sick. But she recovered eventually. She is off with Richard today, and Cass is meeting Liz, who is going off to the Gaeltacht on Monday morning. But we are having a band practice tomorrow, and afterwards Cass is calling over to my house to stay the night, because we can do that sort of thing on a Sunday night during the holidays. (Alice can't come because she has to be up early on Monday to go on one of her family's regular visits to some random relations.) So, in the meantime, I have a whole day of freedom to myself.

LATER

I can't actually think of anything to do.

LATER

I think I will just go and sit in the garden and read for a bit. The one good thing about the summer is that, even if you are a bit bored, you can be bored in the sun. Which is nice.

LATER

I am still bored. I'm just not in the mood for lying in the sun and reading. It is very unfair. For ages I've been dreaming about being able to just lie around and read, and now I can do it, I don't actually feel like it. I said this to Mum, and she said that life was often like that, and, if I was really bored, I could help her clean out under the stairs.

I should have known better than to say I was bored to Mum. Parents never understand that if you're bored, doing something horrible like going through ancient boxes of old wellies will just make you even more bored. I think I will sneak out and go for a walk around the block and listen to my iPod. At least some fresh air and exercise will do me good.

LATER

Still bored. I give up. I might as well help Mum sort out boxes of wellies. How has my life come to this?

LATER

The wellies that still fit members of the family (one pair each) have been matched up neatly under the stairs. The rest are in a bin bag ready to be thrown away. That is today's greatest achievement, which says something about how boring my life is at the moment. I actually feel a bit bad about just chucking the wellies away – after all, I have spent two years hearing Miss Kelly go on about the importance of looking after the environment and not adding to giant landfill dumps. But I don't think a charity shop would want our manky old wellies with holes in them. And Mum said she didn't think there is anywhere that recycles wellies. There probably should be, though.

SUNDAY ☼

Band practice today! Luckily my mum and dad were going to some garden centre out in Malahide and said they'd drop me and Cass off at Alice's on the way there. It was great to be able to practise without having to worry about exams or school stuff. (I still have the nagging worry about Patricia Alexandra

Harrington in Mum's book, but it's easier to forget about that now I know I don't have to see Mrs Harrington on Monday. So I just won't think about it for a while. I have a feeling that this is not actually a very sensible attitude to life's problems, but it'll do for now.)

Anyway, the practice went pretty well. It might be our last practice before the rock school starts, so we wanted to make sure that we're well prepared. I mean, I know we're going there to learn the ways of rock, but we don't want everyone else, including our mentor (whoever he or she is), to think we're totally hopeless.

Oops, the doorbell just rang, so I think Cass has arrived – she had to go home and get her overnight stuff because she forgot to bring it to Alice's house. I just hope my parents manage to refrain from singing anything from *Oliver!* while she is here.

MONDAY ☀

Wow. Cass has just gone home, and she had some very big news. I feel a bit stunned. But not in a bad way.

I'd better start at the beginning. We all got a posh takeaway which was very nice even though we had to eat it with my parents. Actually, they were unusually well behaved, and took themselves off to the dining room to practise their *Oliver!* songs as soon as dinner was over (well, I suppose they were only relatively well behaved – we could still hear them through the walls) so Cass and I could have the telly and the DVD player to ourselves. Eventually, they basically booted us upstairs to my room – they wanted the sitting room back so my mother could watch one of the ridiculous crime programmes she's so fond of. It was quite late by then so we got into our pyjamas and blew up the air mattress and made up Cass's bed on it so we could loll about in more comfort. Then we got talking about the summer and the camp and everything. But Cass started to seem a bit down.

'Are you okay?' I said (as you can see, I am still sticking to the rule I made in February to pay attention to my friends' problems and not be too self-obsessed).

Cass sighed.

'Yeah,' she said. 'Well, sort of. I'm just ... well, you know Liz is going to the Gaeltacht tomorrow?'

'Yeah,' I said.

'Well, I'm just going to really miss her,' said Cass. 'I mean,

I'm not going to see her for three whole weeks. It seems like forever.'

'It's only three weeks,' I said.

'Well, it's going to feel like longer. I wish she wasn't going.'

I was starting to feel a bit insulted.

'Cass,' I said, 'I know Liz is your friend, but you do have other friends who are still here, you know. I mean, it's not like she's your girlfriend and your own true love or anything!'

I expected Cass to say, 'Yeah, I know,' but instead there was a longer than usual silence. And then Cass, in a slightly strained voice, said, 'Well ... she sort of is. My girlfriend, I mean.'

I was so surprised I didn't say anything for a moment. I don't even know why I was so amazed – it's not like I don't know any gay people. Mum's friend Maria, who lives around the corner, is gay, and so are some of my parents' other friends. But, despite this, I suppose I just take it for granted that everyone, including Cass, is straight. Which, now I think of it, is a bit silly, because obviously not everyone is. I mean, it turns out Cass isn't.

'Bex?' said Cass. 'Didn't you hear? I basically just told you I'm gay.'

'Oh!' I said. 'Yes! I did! Sorry. I was just a bit surprised.

But … really? Wow.'

'Yes,' said Cass. There was silence for a moment, and then she said, 'Are you … you're okay with it, right?'

'Oh God, yes!' I said. 'Of course I am! I just wasn't expecting it.' And then I was worried that I was saying the wrong thing and upsetting Cass. 'Sorry, Cass. I really am okay with it. I'm more than okay. It's cool. I'm just a bit surprised.'

'Really?' said Cass. 'I actually thought it was getting kind of obvious. Especially recently.'

'Well, not to me,' I said. 'But maybe I am quite clueless.' I really think I must be. 'Um, so are you and Liz, like, actually properly going out?'

'Only since last weekend,' said Cass. 'I would have told you sooner, but there were, you know, the exams and stuff. But anyway, I've liked her for ages. Ever since we met, really. She told me she was gay a few weeks ago, and then last weekend we were in her house, and we were talking about, like, life and how things have been for her since she came out. She's had a bit of a tough time because when she came out to Katie, you know, her bandmate from Bad Monkey, Katie was really weird about it for a while. Though things are a bit better now. I mean, they're still going to the Gaeltacht together and everything. Anyway, Liz said something sort-of-jokey about how she wished I liked girls too. And I said that actually, I did, and we sort of looked at each other, and then she kissed me ... and that was it, really. She said she's liked me for ages too, but she was never sure whether I even fancied girls at all, let alone fancied her.'

'Wow,' I said. 'How romantic. But Cass, why didn't you tell me or Alice sooner? Not about you and Liz, I know the whole week has been about exams. I mean, why did you never tell us that you like girls? We're your best friends!' I have to admit, I felt hurt.

'I know you are,' said Cass. 'But I didn't know how you'd react.'

I felt quite insulted by that.

'Cass, how could you have thought I'd be horrible about it? I'm not homophobic!'

And Cass looked, not exactly annoyed, but much more serious than she generally looks. 'Bex, I do know you're cool with it, and I'm very relieved that you are, and it's not like I really expected you to be anything else, not really.' She sighed. 'But there was always a chance that you wouldn't be okay. I mean, people can be fine about gayness in theory, but not in, like, practice. If you know what I mean. That's what happened with Liz and Katie.'

'Yeah,' I said. 'I see what you mean.'

'I mean,' Cass went on, warming to the theme, 'it may not seem like it to you, but this is a really, really big deal. Me, you know, coming out to you. It was really scary. I've basically been dreading it for ages. I ... I dunno. I was scared that if I told you, things would never be the same, and we wouldn't be normal friends anymore or maybe even friends at all, and I was really scared about that.'

She looked like she might cry. And I almost felt like bursting into tears myself.

But I just gave Cass a hug (which shows what an emotional moment it was, we're not usually terribly huggy). And we both sniffled back tears.

Anyway, after that we stayed up talking about it for ages, and I tried to say the right thing, though I'm not sure I always did. But I wanted to, anyway. And she didn't seem to mind. I think once she knew I was cool with it and that I appreciated what a big deal it was for her to tell me, everything was okay between us. She said she'd fancied girls for as long as she'd fancied anyone.

'But only in, like, theory,' she said. 'I mean, the famous people I fancied were girls. I never met anyone I really liked in real life until I met Liz.'

'Which isn't really surprising when you look around in our school,' I said. 'Imagine anyone falling in love with Vanessa. But I remember you saying how good-looking Paperboy and Jack Rosenthal from *Laurel Canyon* are! Were you just pretending? You never needed to do that!'

But she said she wasn't, really.

'I'm gay,' she said. 'But I'm not blind. Obviously I can appreciate, you know, when someone's really good-looking, whether they're a boy or a girl.'

She still hasn't told her mum and dad. She's really nervous about it.

'I can't imagine them being upset about it,' I said. 'I mean, it's not like they're really anti-gay, or anything. Isn't your mum friends with my mum's friend Maria?'

'But people can be one way about their friends and another way about their kids,' said Cass. 'I dunno. Imagine how awful it would be if Mum didn't get it. Like, if she thought it was just a phase. Or if she, like, cried with sorrow.'

And I realised it was easy for me to say that everything

would be okay. As long as there was a chance that it wouldn't, poor Cass would be very nervous about it.

'Yeah, I understand,' I said, and I think I did. 'When are you going to tell Alice?'

'Tomorrow, I hope,' said Cass. 'Oh, no, she's doing more family stuff, isn't she? Well, Tuesday, then. I'll text her tomorrow and arrange to meet her. I was actually going to tell both of you together, but I suppose it just ... came out tonight.'

'Like yourself,' I said, and we both laughed like loons even though that was not one of my finest jokes. It was good to laugh after all that seriousness, though. And then we realised it was nearly two in the morning, and we were both kind of knackered, so we went to bed.

'I feel quite exhausted after all that soul-bearing,' said Cass, through a giant yawn.

'So do I,' I said. 'I'm glad you told me, though.'

'Me too,' said Cass. 'Night night.'

At first I thought I would lie there pondering Cass's announcement. But actually, I fell asleep straight away. Cass is right, those sort of conversations are very tiring. Anyway, I didn't get to sleep very long because the noise my dad makes banging around the house in the morning would wake anyone up. Why he makes so much noise just getting ready to go and correct some exams is beyond me. It's not like he's, like, a carpenter and has to gather together lots of noisy spanners and hammers and stuff. Anyway, he woke us both up by slamming the bathroom door by accident, which happens almost every morning, and we sat up and looked at each other. Well, we sort of looked at each other; Cass can't focus very well without her glasses.

'Did you tell me you were gay last night or was that just a magical dream?' I said.

'It wasn't a magical dream,' said Cass, putting on her glasses. There was a slightly awkward pause. 'Um, you're still okay about it all, aren't you?'

'No,' I said. 'I have turned into a lesbian-hater overnight. I'm joking! Sorry! That wasn't very funny. I am definitely still okay about it.'

'Good,' said Cass. 'Can we talk about other stuff now? Even I am getting slightly bored talking about myself.'

'We could talk about our sweet-making plans,' I said.

'Ooh, yes,' said Cass. 'Do you think your mum would let us try again?'

She said we could try again, but there was no condensed

milk or indeed sugar left so we'd have to go out and buy some. So we did, after breakfast, and then we went back to my house and made some more fudge. I think we are really getting the hang of it – it was much better than the last batch. Even Rachel grudgingly admitted that it wasn't bad, which is a lot coming from her. So by the time Cass had to go home (with an old plastic takeaway box filled with half of the batch of fudge), we were feeling very pleased with ourselves. When I walked her out to the door it felt a bit formal for a second.

'Well,' I said, 'um, thanks for telling me. You know, last night.'

'Oh, yeah,' said Cass. 'Um, thanks for ... listening?'

And then we started laughing, and everything was normal again. And then she went home. And now I am writing this. Although I'd better stop, I can hear my dad calling me. He probably wants to me to do the hoovering or some other servant-like duty.

LATER

I have just realised something. Now Alice is going out with Richard and Cass is going out with Liz, I am the only one of the three of us who isn't going out with anyone! I know I shouldn't feel bad about this, but I sort of do. It's not that I feel I really need a boyfriend, but I'm starting to wonder if I will ever find love again. Maybe I will meet someone at the rock camp, although the last time I met a boy while doing some sort of creative activity it was John Kowalski, and look how that turned out. Perhaps I will just be on my own for the rest of my life. That makes me feel a bit crap.

LATER

I have written a poem about my loveless state:

> *All of my best friends*
> *Have got boyfriends or girlfriends*
> *Frankly it's not fair.*

I have a feeling this poem makes me look a bit selfish. I know I should just be happy for the others. But I do kind of feel like this.

TUESDAY ☾

Cass told Alice today. Alice rang me later to tell me, and it seems it didn't all go exactly as planned. They met up in town and went to the Pepperpot Café for hot chocolate. Alice says she was a bit worried because Cass seemed much more serious than usual. And when they were sitting down, Cass said, 'So ... I've got something to tell you.'

I have no idea why, but Alice was somehow immediately convinced that it was, well, a matter of life or death. She says she was practically in tears as she said, 'Oh Cass, no – do you have cancer? Are you ... dying?'

Cass, understandably, stared at her in amazement.

'What?' she said. 'No! I'm fine! Oh God, Alice, don't cry all over your hot chocolate, you'll make it all salty and gross. I'm not dying. I'm gay!'

'Oh, thank God!' said Alice.

Anyway, they both realised that this was pretty funny, so things were okay after that, and they drank the nice hot chocolate and then went off and looked at amps in a music shop.

'Did it ever cross your mind?' said Alice when she rang me

to tell me about it (Cass had told her about coming out to me the night before), 'That Cass liked girls, I mean?'

'No,' I admitted. 'I never thought about it.'

'Me neither,' said Alice. 'I just assumed she was straight. Like I assumed you were.'

'Me too,' I said. 'You are okay with it, aren't you?'

'Oh God, yes,' said Alice. 'I mean, I was surprised when she told me. But it's not like she's any different, is she? I mean, she's still the same Cass. It's not like it means she fancies any of us. So what difference does it make? I'm mostly just sad she didn't tell us before.'

'Me too,' I said. 'But at least she's told us now.'

And it's true, it doesn't make a difference. I mean, obviously I was thinking about it when she was telling me. But in the morning, when we were making fudge and stuff, it wasn't ... an issue. I mean, I can hardly spend all my time imagining my friends' love lives, can I? That would be pretty creepy.

I didn't mention to Alice that I feel a bit bad about being the only single one of us three. I knew it would sound very babyish and selfish. But I do feel like that, even though most of our other friends aren't going out with anyone either. It's different when it's your very best friends.

WEDNESDAY ❧

I have decided I am going to do something daring to get out of this blah mood. I am going to get my hair cut and finally get a fringe, so when we start the summer camp next week I will look like a new and exciting person. I have been dreaming of having a fringe for years, but I haven't got one because of my weird wavy hair. But I bet hairdressing techniques have improved a LOT since the long-ago days when I last had a fringe and it just kept sticking out like a shelf. I mean, it was years ago AND I was a very small child at the time. I told Cass about my plan today.

'Are you sure about this?' she said. 'You've always been sure you couldn't have a fringe. It's a big commitment. And it can go horribly wrong.'

'But you have a fringe!' I said.

'I know,' said Cass. 'But remember, I've had one for years. I was trying to grow it out for ages and ages until I finally just gave in and accepted it. Fringes can be tricky things. And your hair is even thicker than mine.'

'But Cass, they can DO things now,' I said. 'I was looking in one of Mum's magazines, and it said if you start the fringe high up on your head, the weight of the hair will keep it straight, even if it's really thick.'

'I suppose,' said Cass. 'It's still risky, though.'

'What's the name of your hairdresser?' I said. 'The one who gave you the proper fringe a few months ago? I want to go to someone who has, like, proved their fringe-cutting skills.'

Cass told me the name. 'But you're not going to get exactly the same style as me, are you?' she said. 'It would look very odd if we turned up at the rock camp as hair twins. Like it was a band uniform.'

'Of course I'm not!' I said. 'Anyway, my hair's much longer than yours. Well, a few inches, anyway. And I'm not going to get much cut off most of it, just the front. You're not the only person who's allowed have a fringe, you know!'

'Okay, okay,' said Cass. 'On your own head be it. Literally,' she added. But I refused to laugh at her terrible jest.

Alice was slightly more supportive of my great reinvention plan. But only slightly.

'Well, if you don't like it, you can grow it out,' she said. She didn't sound as if she thought I actually would like it, though.

Anyway, perhaps in the past I would have been persuaded by all of this, but somehow it has just made me even more determined to do it. I asked Mum if she'd give me money to get my hair cut and she said she would.

'It could do with a bit of a trim, you've got some split ends,' she said, rudely. Really, she has no manners. I told her about my fringe plan, and she liked the idea, though not for a particularly good reason.

'You looked lovely with your fringe when you were little,' she said. This is a total lie, obviously. But maybe it just means I will look brilliant with a proper fringe as a sophisticated teenager?

THURSDAY ◎

Quite a nice lazy day today. The weather was really nice so I spent ages just lying out in the back garden on a blanket, reading and listening to Best Coast on my iPod. I was actually in the mood for it, unlike Saturday. I generally like lazing around doing nothing when I know I could actually go and do something if I really wanted to. It's just boring when you feel you don't have a choice. I was reading a brilliant book called *Howl's Moving Castle*. It's set in a magical world, and the heroine is a teenage girl who gets turned into a hideous old lady, but, although that sounds pretty grim, it is very funny and exciting.

Anyway, I won't have much time to laze around like this next week because I will be rocking at the rock camp all day, so I am enjoying it while I can. And tomorrow I am getting my hair cut. I am a bit nervous but I have a good feeling about it. I flicked over some of my hair in front of my forehead to make it look like a fringe today and I think it really suited me. And that was just a fake fringe! Surely a real one will be even better.

FRIDAY ☺

I have a fringe! And it is all sleek and flat and I love it! I look like a whole new glamorous person. I was a bit nervous in the hairdresser's this morning when she started chopping off the front of my hair and I could see long locks of it falling on my lap, but she spent ages trimming and shaping and spraying and drying it and when it was all finished I just stared at my reflection in amazement.

'Do you like it?' said the hairdresser, whose name was Cliona.

'I love it!' I said. And I did. I can't remember when I'd ever actually felt so pleased after getting my hair cut. Usually I'm just relieved it hasn't all gone horribly wrong. I met Cass, Alice and Jane afterwards, and Cass had to eat her words.

'Okay, okay,' she said. 'You were right. It does look good. Cliona has worked her magic.'

'You look kind of French,' said Alice, 'which is a good thing. Like you should be scooting around Paris on a moped.'

'Welcome to the world of fringes,' said Jane, who has always had a nice, well-behaved fringe.

'I'm starting to feel left out,' said Alice. 'Maybe I should get one too?'

'Then we really would look like we had band hair,' said Cass.

'True,' said Alice. 'Okay, I won't.'

Alice has trouble-free hair anyway, thanks to her mum, who has blonde shiny locks which Alice has inherited. Both she and Jane always look very well put together, unlike me. I always seem to be a tiny bit scruffy. But not anymore! Now I have my French Girl Fringe. Even Rachel admitted it looked good when I got home.

'Wow,' she said. 'That really suits you.'

'You don't have to sound so surprised,' I said.

'God, can't you take a compliment gracefully?' she said, and stomped off. But she's just in a bad mood because her saintly boyfriend Tom is going on holiday with his parents tomorrow. Even Mum making a delicious casserole for dinner didn't cheer her up.

SATURDAY ☺

OH MY GOD. Something terrible has happened. I went out to Alice's house for a band practice today (which went very well, not that it matters now because I will never be leaving the house again, so I suppose the band is over). When Cass and I were waiting for the bus to get home, it started to rain, and we got totally soaked. Like, all my clothes were wet right down to my underwear, which is pretty revolting. Anyway, I squelched home from my bus stop in my sopping Converse and changed into my pyjamas and towelled off my hair. My hair was almost dry, and I was starting to feel normal again when I went to the loo and caught sight of myself in the mirror over the sink.

I was so horrified I actually shrieked, and my mum came running upstairs to see what was wrong.

'Look at my hair!' I cried.

'Oh for God's sake, Rebecca, don't scream like that,' said Mum. 'I thought you'd had a terrible accident.'

'But look at it!' I said. I couldn't believe it. Basically, it turns out that the only thing that was keeping my fringe all flat and shiny was all the blow-drying and styling products from the hairdresser's yesterday. Now it has gone back to its natural state, and it is just like my childhood fringe! Except I think it's actually worse because my hair seems to have got much thicker since then!

'It's just a bit ... fluffy,' said Mum.

'It's bushy!' I said. 'It's like a bushy mop!' My hair has always had bushy-mop tendencies, of course, but at least when it's long the weight of the hair keeps it fairly flat. But now the fringe was just sticking out wildly. I didn't look like a cool French girl anymore. I looked like someone out of a 1980s film with giant pouffy hair.

And then, of course, Rachel came in and started laughing.

'Wow, the eighties revival has started in this house,' she said. 'That's some big hair.'

'Shut up!' I said. 'It went funny in the rain.'

'It certainly did,' said Rachel. And I couldn't bear looking at her horrible laughing face for another second so I ran off to my room. But even there my torment continued (and not just because I could see myself and my ridiculous hair in the mirror on my dressing table). That evil Mulligan kid was in her room, and when she saw me she started laughing and put her hands up on her head as if she was puffing up a giant mane of hair! I hate her so much.

And now someone is knocking at my door. Can't the world leave me alone in my misery for a minute?

LATER

Okay, maybe Rachel isn't totally evil. She got her hair straighteners and lots of anti-frizz serum and tried to calm my hair again. It looked slightly better when she'd tried her magic, and it's not wavy anymore, but it's still sticking out quite a bit. Also, I get quite nervous having those hot straighteners right next to my eyes. It feels a bit dangerous. I don't think you're meant to use them on fringes. Anyway, I still look ridiculous. Cass rang to see about meeting up tomorrow, and I had to tell her what had happened. To her great credit she didn't actually say 'I told you so.' She just expressed sympathy and said she'd try and fix it tomorrow, using her years of fringe-battling experience. Maybe the freedom of coming out has made her a more noble person?

SUNDAY ☼

Huh, so much for Cass becoming more noble. As soon as I arrived at her house today and she actually saw my stupid fringe, she said, 'Yikes! Well, I did tell you not to do it.'

'Cass!' I said. 'That's not very helpful.'

'No, it's not,' said Alice. 'Come on, Cass. Use your magic anti-fringe powers!'

'Oh, all right,' said Cass. 'Sorry, Bex.'

Anyway, I suppose she redeemed herself by trying to make my hair look normal again. She said that when a fringe is really misbehaving there's no point in trying to flatten it out.

'You've just got to pretend it doesn't exist,' she said. 'This is where hair pins come in.'

Then she and Alice spent about five years fussing over my hair. I seem to have spent most of the last few days having my head poked at. Anyway, they tried several methods. After I begged them to try flattening it anyway, they tried calming it down with more serum, but it started to just go all greasy and icky. Then they scraped it straight back from my face, but that didn't work either.

'I think it just highlights my unsymmetrical face,' I said miserably.

Then they pouffed up the front in a sort of quiff.

'That looks quite good,' said Alice kindly.

'Though,' said Cass. 'Um. It also makes you look a tiny bit like Vanessa. She does that with her hair.'

'Try something else!' I cried.

Eventually they sort of pulled it back and to the side, so it looked softer and not so scraped.

'It does need quite a few pins,' said Alice.

'But I think it works,' said Cass. 'Doesn't it?'

I suppose it does. I took all the pins out and tried to do it myself (it's not like I'm going to have Cass and Alice around every day to be my personal hairdressers), and it looked a bit wonky but not too bad. Better than a giant eighties pouffy fringe, anyway. I tried washing my hair again when I got home and putting in lots of posh conditioner, but it didn't make any difference; my fringe was still all big with a kink in it. They must have magical powers in that stupid hairdresser's, I can't see how they made it look normal for twenty-four hours.

So much for my dream of arriving at the summer camp with a glamorous new look, anyway. I'm now more likely to spend the entire thing wearing a hat. Though what sort of hat could I wear? If only it were a winter camp, then I could wear a beret or something and it wouldn't look too bad. But most people don't wear hats in the summer, do they? Unless they're on a beach. I can hardly go around the college wearing a giant floppy sun hat. I'll just have to spend this evening practising with my new packet of hair pins. Why did I ever think it was a good idea to get a stupid fringe? Everyone should have talked me out of it!

MONDAY ☼

I had to get up really early today to deal with my stupid fringe. I hoped it might have got nice and flat and sleek overnight, but it hasn't. It still looks all puffy. So I tried to reproduce what Cass and Alice did last night, and, although it took ages and a lot of fiddling around with pins, I think it worked. It didn't look totally freakish anyway. And I used Rachel's brilliant mineral powder and my nice new posh lipstick so people would notice that instead of my weird hair.

Though to be honest, today was so much fun I actually forgot about my fringe after a while. This morning I met up with Alice, Cass and Richard, and we all walked down to the college together. The actual campus was huge, with loads of different buildings, which was all very confusing, and we ended up wandering around in circles until we found a 'North Dublin Summer Arts Camp this way' sign.

'You'd think they'd have put these signs near the actual gates,' said Cass grumpily. But she only sounded grumpy because she was feeling a bit nervous. As was I. I don't even know why.

Anyway, we followed the sign and ended up at one of the biggest buildings. Seriously, it was about the size of our whole school, and it was just for arts stuff. And there's a theatre somewhere on the campus as well.

When we went inside, there were loads of boys and girls milling around looking as confused as we felt. Lots of them looked a bit older than us, which made me feel even more nervous. But eventually we found a big noticeboard telling us where all the different groups were meeting up. All the bands were told to go to the Orchestra Room.

'Orchestra Room!' said Cass. 'That sounds very fancy.'

It wasn't, though. It was just a big room with a grand piano and some chairs in it and loads of music stands piled up in a corner. We all sat down and looked around at our fellow summer-schoolers.

'I wonder will we be able to find Jane and Ellie at lunch?' I said.

'I was wondering the same thing,' said Alice. 'This place seems huge. I can't imagine we'll ever be able to find our way around it.'

'Consider it practice for when we get to actual college,' said Richard, but he looked very relieved a minute later when his bandmates came in. He waved at them, and they came over and grabbed some seats nearby. We didn't know any of the other bands, but one of them included a few boys from Richard's class in school. He didn't seem to like them very much and with good reason.

'I didn't realise they were doing this,' he said when he noticed them on the other side of the hall.

'Is their band any good?' I asked.

'I doubt it,' said Richard. 'Ah, I dunno, I'm not being fair.

They could be good. They're just kind of ... annoying.'

But before he could say anything else, a man and a woman walked up to a pair of microphones set up next to the grand piano and waved. Everyone suddenly stopped talking.

'Wow,' said the woman, looking a bit surprised. 'You're all very quiet all of a sudden! So ... hi! My name's Veronica Flaherty, and I'm a guitarist and a sound engineer.'

Cass and Alice and I looked at each other. Veronica had been one of the organisers of the Battle of the Bands!

'And my name is Tom, and I play the bass,' said the man, 'and sometimes the drums.'

Then Veronica told us how excited they were about the summer arts school and gave a speech about what we'd be doing over the next three weeks, which we kind of knew already from the website, and how at the end of it we'd put on shows for everyone in the camp. Then she called in all the people who were going to be our mentors, which sounds very reality TV. There were four men and two women, and they all looked like they were in their twenties and thirties. Some of them looked quite familiar – the camp has managed to get some quite big bands, which is impressive. When a very tall skinny man in a sharp suit came out, Richard looked very surprised and excited.

'No one's going to try and make you sound a certain way,' said Veronica. 'We're just going to help you do the stuff you already want to do.' The mentors each introduced themselves, and there was more talking about what we were going to do in each week, and then we were released into the wild, or at least the rest of the college, for a short break. As soon as Veronica and Tom left the stage, Richard said, 'Oh my God, did you see who that was?'

'Who who was?' said Alice.

'It was Ian Cliff! In the suit! Ian Cliff from Verfremdungseffekt!' said Richard.

'Oh yeah,' said Alice. 'They're not bad.'

Verfremdungseffekt are a Dublin band who are pretty popular, and Richard loves them. Alice went with him to one of their gigs a while ago and said they were pretty good, in a sort of melodramatic gloomy kind of way (which, now I think of it, is quite like Richard's own band).

'What does Verfremd-whatsit actually mean?' I said. 'It sounds a bit German.'

'It is German,' said Alice. Her mum is German so Alice can speak German better than our actual German teacher. 'It literally means, like, alienation effect. Or distancing effect. But I don't know what that really means. If you know what I mean.'

We did.

But Richard, because he is Verfremdungseffekt's biggest fan ever, did know what alienation effect meant.

'There was a German writer called Brecht who did plays, and he wanted to remind the audiences that they were actually watching a play, not real people, so they'd be more critical and not get emotionally involved. So *Verfremdungseffekt* is the word he used to describe how he did this. The characters would, like, turn around and start talking to the audience and stuff.'

I was not very impressed by this. I don't think I've ever forgotten that I was watching a play. I mean, surely it's quite obvious that the people are, like, on a stage? And acting? Anyway, Richard was still going out about how brilliant Ian Cliff was and how much he hoped they'd get him as their mentor when we left the Orchestra Room. And it turned out that we needn't have worried about not finding anyone because as soon as we walked out into the corridor we bumped into Jane.

'Oh, thank God I've found you,' said Jane. 'Something terrible has happened.'

'Oh God, you're not sick, are you?' said Alice nervously.

'No,' said Jane. 'Well, sort of. But only because they divided us up into groups, and I'm in the same one as Vanessa and Karen! And Bernard the Fairy-tale Prince, though I don't really have anything against him apart from the fact he's going out with Karen. We're going to have to spend the whole summer camp coming up with a play together.'

'Just the four of you?' said Alice.

'No, thank God,' said Jane. 'There's another girl and two boys. But still!'

'Oh dear,' I said. And I patted her arm sympathetically.

'Oh well,' said Jane bravely. 'It'll be good acting practice, trying to pretend they're not driving me mad. What's your thing like?'

'Pretty good, I think,' said Cass. And we told her about Veronica and Tom and the mentors.

'So, who's your mentor?' said Jane.

'We don't know yet,' I said. 'They're telling us in a few minutes when we go back in. Do you have mentors?'

'Not like that,' said Jane. 'Just facilitators. Whatever that means, exactly. Oh! I forgot to tell you. One of them is Cathy.'

'Director Cathy?' said Alice. Cathy Laverty directed our

production of *Mary Poppins*. She was okay, in an intimidating, serious sort of way.

'The very same,' said Jane. 'She's still doing that scary glare thing. One of the boys started messing around at the start of the session, and she just ... stared at him until he turned around, and then he shut up immediately. It's like magic.'

Then we realised that people were starting to go back into the various meeting rooms, so we told Jane we'd see her at lunch and headed back into the Orchestra Room. When we got back to our seats, Richard and his bandmates had been joined by the other band from their school. They were having a serious conversation about which mentor they wanted to get. Of course Richard was going on about Ian Cliff and how he was the greatest artist in Dublin and Verfremdungseffekt were the best band since the Bad Seeds.

'Yeah, they're not bad,' said a boy from the other band. He laughed. 'We'll have to fight you lot for him.'

'I hope we don't get one of the girls,' said one of his bandmates. 'I just can't take girly musicians seriously.' He looked at us and grinned in what he probably thought was a charming way but which looked more like a smirk to me. 'No offence.'

'Lots of offence taken,' I said. I could see why Richard

hadn't looked very pleased to see them here. He looked even less pleased now.

'Wow, Charlie,' said Richard. 'I didn't realise you were that scared of girls.'

Charlie looked annoyed.

'I'm not SCARED of them, Murray,' he said. But before he could say anything else obnoxious, Veronica and Tom and the mentors came back in.

'So,' said Tom. 'We're going to give you each a mentor now! First up ... Richard Murray and the Wicked Ways. Where are you, Wicked Ways?'

Richard and the bandmates put up their hands and looked a bit nervous.

'Your mentor is Ian Cliff from Verfremdungseffekt!' said Tom, and Richard looked very relieved. Ian looked over and nodded at them in a very serious way.

Then they called the Crack Parrots, which, it turns out, is the name of horrible Charlie's band. I was hoping he'd get one of the women but alas he didn't, he got some man called Simon from a band called Aniseed. And then it was our turn.

'Now, where are Hey Dollface? Ah, hello there,' said Veronica. 'Your mentor is Kitty Shorthall from the Chalet School!'

A woman with a bob and a very cool dress gave us a cheerful wave. We waved back, and Veronica went through the rest of the list. There were seven bands and, to our surprise, one solo artist.

'Right, last but not least is Paula Howard,' said Veronica. 'Our only solo act this year. Where are you, Paula?'

A very small girl all dressed in black with lots of hair and a fringe that almost covered her eyes put up her hand.

'Cool,' said Veronica. 'Your mentor is Dave Crewe from Panda Gun. Right, now I want you all to come up here and meet your mentors! And then you'll go off for your first workshops. Today you're going to have workshops with your mentors all day, but from tomorrow we'll be mixing things up a little.'

'See you later then,' said Richard, giving Alice a quick kiss, and then we all went off to find our mentors.

'What if she hates us?' said Cass.

'What if we hate her?' I said.

'Oh, don't be silly,' said Alice. 'She'll be lovely. She looks nice and friendly.'

And she was all of these things. Unlike obnoxious Charlie, I wanted us to get a woman for a mentor. There aren't really that many girls in bands like ours, and it's surprising what a difference it makes when you actually see any. It's like you've got permission to do what you're doing, even though you know that really you never needed any permission. Kitty seemed to feel the same way.

'Hello, ladies,' she said when we came up and introduced ourselves. 'I'm really glad I got a band with girls in it. It's always good to see more girls starting bands!'

And after that we got on really well. We went into our designated practice room, which had some amps and instruments in it, and Kitty told us about her band, the Chalet School, which sounds really cool; they met when they were in college, and they released their first album last year. And, of course, we told her all about Hey Dollface.

'We played our first gig at the Battle of the Bands in the Knitting Factory last year,' said Cass. 'It went pretty well.'

I was going to say, 'Apart from the bit where I fell backwards off the drum platform,' but then I stopped myself. Surely Kitty didn't need to know about that minor mishap? It wasn't like I'm going to do it again. At least, I hope not.

'But we had to take a break for a while because I hurt my wrist,' said Alice. 'So we haven't actually played any shows since then. We want to, though.'

'That's a great idea,' said Kitty. 'And it's great that you've played a gig already. My band were together for about a year before we actually got on a stage!'

It was really easy to talk to her. In fact, I wish she was going to teach us everything, but it turns out that some of the workshops are just going to be each band alone with their mentor, and some of them will be all the bands together. Anyway, we had lots of fun; we played her our song 'The Real Me', and she said it reminded her of a band called Veronica Falls, and before we knew it, it was lunchtime.

'This is brilliant,' I said, as we walked into the big college canteen café place where we're going to have lunch every day. 'We'll probably have written a whole album by the time this course is over!'

'I don't know about that,' said Alice.

'Oh, come on, Alice,' said Cass. 'All this practice! Hours a day! We'll be practically professionals! Ooh, look, there's Jane and Ellie, they've saved us some seats. And who's that with Ellie?'

'It's Sam!' I said. 'From *Mary Poppins*. I don't know who the other red-haired girl is, though.'

'Jane!' roared Cass. 'Ah, she heard us.'

We hurried over.

'Look who it is!' said Ellie. 'Sam's doing the art course too!'

'Hey!' said Sam in a cheerful way.

It was cool to see him again. He had been quite shy for most of the musical, but it turned out that this was because of his terrible fear of having to understudy John Kowalski's stupid part. Anyway, we talked properly for the first time on the very last night of the show, and he turned out to be really nice.

'And this is Lucy,' said Sam, pointing to the red-haired girl. She was very tall and quite imposing, with high cheekbones.

'Hey,' she said, waving at us. We waved back. Then I realised who she was.

'Oh, you do comics together, don't you?' I said. 'Sam told me about them when we were doing the musical.'

'Yeah, that's right,' said Lucy. 'Hello.'

'Cool,' I said. But Lucy didn't say anything else. She just smiled a bit distantly and looked down at her hands. I am not sure if she's rude or shy. There is a fine line sometimes.

Anyway, the art course sounds really good. Cass thought so too. In fact, she is a bit jealous of our artist chums.

'I'm starting to wish we could do a bit of both courses,' she said, as Ellie and Sam explained about their teachers and how they were all going to work on different projects – Ellie's going to do fashion-design stuff, and Sam and Lucy are going to do comics. 'It might be good for my theatre-set-design career.'

But I think we're both glad that we're doing the rock camp. It really is so much fun. And it looks like we'll be able to avoid Vanessa and Karen fairly easily. We only saw them once today, when we were on our way out with Richard.

'What are you doing here?' said Vanessa in her usual charming and not-at-all-rude fashion.

'We're doing the rock camp,' said Cass.

'Oh, right,' said Vanessa. 'I didn't know.'

'Um, you're the one who told us about it,' said Alice.

'Did I?' said Vanessa, in a bored voice. Then she noticed Richard and said, 'Oh, hey, Bert. So you're doing this rock thing too.'

Richard looked confused for a minute.

'Um, it's Richard,' he said. 'I just played Bert in *Mary Poppins*.'

'Richard? Really?' said Vanessa. 'Oh, whatever. I just saw the role, not the boy.' And she marched off, leaving us staring at each other. I can't believe she played the lead role of the musical opposite Richard for weeks and weeks and she can't even remember what his name is.

Oh God, my mother's roaring at me, I'd better go and see what she wants.

LATER

I don't believe it! Apparently even during my actual summer holidays when I am spending my days working hard on the future of music, I am not allowed to relax. Apparently my mother has a problem with me leaving my bag on the floor in the hall. I am not sure where else I'm meant to put it. It's not like there's a special bag cupboard. She also gave out to me for leaving my jacket on the couch instead of hanging it up on the coat rack, which is a bit much if you ask me. It's not like anyone was trying to sit on the bit of the couch where the jacket was. Anyway, I am too fatigued after all that arguing to write much more. But basically we spent the afternoon working on one of our songs with Kitty. It was brilliant, and I actually felt I was learning something. Which is something that doesn't happen in actual school that often.

TUESDAY ☾

Ugh, that boy Charlie and his stupid band Crack Parrots are so disgusting. They were hanging around the main foyer this morning when Ellie, Alice, Cass and I walked in, and when we passed them Charlie pointed at each of us in an obnoxious fashion and said, 'Seven, eight, seven and ...' – he pointed at Cass – 'seven, but if you lost the glasses you might be an eight.'

'What are you talking about?' said Alice.

Charlie smirked, which seems to be his normal facial expression. 'Marks out of ten, girls,' he said. 'But don't worry, you didn't do too badly. I mean, I'd go with any of you if I had to.'

We just stared at him in disgust while his idiot bandmates sniggered. And then we walked off.

'I think we should have said something to him and totally put him in his place,' said Cass. 'But I couldn't think of anything.'

'Neither could I,' I said gloomily. 'What a pig.'

'My mum always says that if someone is rude you should never respond with rudeness,' said Ellie. 'Because the laws of the universe mean that whatever someone sends out into the world is returned to them threefold. Which supposedly means

that if anyone is horrible, they'll get three times as much hor-
ribleness and bad luck back to them. But I'm not sure this is
actually true.'

We looked back at Charlie. He and his stupid friends were
still hanging around making comments at some other girls
who had just come in.

'He looks pretty happy,' said Alice. 'And Richard says he's
always been like that.'

'And think of Vanessa,' said Cass. 'I don't think the universe
has punished her yet either.'

So much for the laws of the universe.

Anyway, besides Charlie and his stupid friends, today was
pretty good. We started writing a new song with Kitty.

'You shouldn't be afraid to mess around,' she said. 'Some of
the best songs happen when you're not trying too hard. Just
fool around with some chords and riffs and see what happens.'

It was very inspiring. We also got talking to some of the
other bands, who seem pretty nice. They are mostly boys, but
there are quite a few girls. There's a girl called Maggie in a
hip-hop group called Positive Trigger who seems cool. And
there's a band called Exquisite Corpse, who are all girls apart
from a boy who plays drums. They are kind of gothy and look

very dramatic and gloomy, but they're not really, as we discovered. When I heard what they were called I thought they were going to be into, like, sitting around in graveyards writing poetry about death, but they turned out to be much more entertaining. We got talking to them when we were in the hall waiting for the afternoon workshops to start. A tall girl with black dyed hair, lots of very dramatic make-up and an amazing sort of corset-y dress that looked very uncomfortable leaned towards us.

'Hiya!' she said, in a very cheerful voice. 'I'm Paula. What d'you think of all this so far?'

She and her bandmates are from Beaumont and are very nice. They practise in her attic.

'My parents were a bit scared at first,' she said. 'I think they thought we'd turned into Satanists or something. They thought we were going up there to do dark rituals. Which we weren't, obviously.'

'They're okay about it now, though,' said her bandmate Sophie. 'Your mam helped me fix my skull hair bobble last week when the skull started coming off the elastic bit.'

'And I think they've got quite into the music,' said Paula. 'I heard my dad humming "Chemical Eternity" the other day.

That's one of our songs,' she added.

'I don't know if that means he likes it, though,' said Sophie. 'It could just be because he's heard it a million times and now it's stuck in his head forever, whether he likes it or not.'

'Yeah, I think my parents are quite relieved we're doing this course,' said Paula. 'It gives us somewhere to practise so we won't be up in the attic for a while.'

'We've got a big shed at my house,' said Alice. She explained about living in the middle of nowhere. 'It should be perfect. But it's tricky for the others to get to. I wish there was somewhere in town we could use.'

It was fun talking to another band about this sort of thing. It's good to know we're not the only ones with organisational problems. They were all really nice. And it turns out even their name isn't that creepy really. It's just what a group of artists used to call that game where you draw a head and fold over the paper and then someone else does the same and draws the body and then someone else draws the legs. So not very scary at all. In fact, Paula is more chirpy than I am, even though she sings songs about falling in love with ghosts.

There is also the other, shorter Paula, Paula Howard, the small solo artist with the fringe. She is very quiet in a mysterious sort of way. Whenever you say anything to her she just answers in very short sentences. But she's not unfriendly. Small Paula is the only solo artist, and no one really knows what her music is like yet. She is quite intriguing. In fact, everyone on the course seems to be doing lots of different things. It's a good mix. We're all going to put on gigs for the whole camp over the last few days of the show, but of course we'll get to see most people do stuff during the workshops over the next few weeks.

But, if I am being very shallow (and surely I should be allowed to be shallow in my own diary), I must admit that I am quite disappointed with the boys. Is that really mean? It's just that I was hoping I might fancy someone, and there isn't really anyone there that I fancy. Even though there are loads of boys on the course. I have a horrible feeling I really will never find love again. Maybe Paperboy and John Kowalski are all I'm ever going to get. And maybe I should be content with that, but I do still want to, like, fall madly in love with someone and not have them leave the country after five minutes or turn out to be a total goon. Surely that's not too much to ask?

Also, my fringe is still misbehaving. I hoped it might have grown a bit in the last few days which might weigh it down some more. But it doesn't seem to have happened. It's still as fluffy as ever. On the plus side, I have got better at clipping it back and to the side so it doesn't look too bad then. But still.

WEDNESDAY ✿

If we are not complete musical experts by the end of this course I will be very surprised. Today we had an excellent songwriting workshop with Richard's beloved Ian Cliff. I do not think he is as much of a genius as Richard does, but he was very good. And very imposing, as he is about ten feet tall in his stylish suits (he always wears suits – I can't imagine him in, like, jeans) and looks even taller because his black hair is pushed up in a sort of quiff. But he has revitalised my creativity, especially when it comes to writing lyrics. Ever since Paperboy's absence fuelled my creative powers, I've ended up becoming the band's chief lyric-writer, but so far I've mostly written lyrics about what I was feeling at that very moment, which is probably why I haven't been feeling very creative lately, what with things being dull and exam-centric.

But Ian Cliff reminded me that we can all draw from our past. And, as my love life seems to be a thing of the past, this was fine by me. So I have come up with some lyrics for the song we started working on yesterday. They are about John Kowalski.

I met you at rehearsal
Your clothes they smelled like Persil
Oh-oh, oh-oh
You went out for a smoke break
And I felt my heart quake
Oh-oh, oh-oh

I think I might have to work on them a bit before I show them to Cass and Alice. I know that Persil line is a bit odd. And I don't even know if John's clothes were washed with Persil. It could have been Daz. Or something environmentally friendly like Ecover (Miss Kelly would approve of that). Anyway, whatever they were washed with, he didn't do the actual washing. He used to boast that he always refused to do what he called 'mundane, pointless household duties', even when his parents threatened to stop his pocket money. He seemed quite outraged at the very idea that he could be 'bought off', as he put it.

Anyway, I wouldn't want to mention anything to do with laundry at all but very few things rhyme with 'rehearsal'. In fact, I couldn't think of anything else. But I'll figure something out.

And I wasn't the only one who has been creative and productive today. When we met Jane at lunch today she had some surprising news – though we were lucky we were able to hear it because Positive Trigger have started having rap battles with each other at lunchtime and sometimes they can get quite heated and noisy (though in quite a good-natured way. I think it's all for show; they all seem to be good friends). Anyway, we managed to find a relatively quiet corner and sat down with some sandwiches.

'How's it going, working with you-know-who?' asked Cass sympathetically. 'Do you have to go out to the corridor every few minutes and take deep breaths to calm down?'

'Do you think you'll get through the whole thing without pushing Karen off the stage?' I said. 'I used to want to do that a lot during *Mary Poppins* rehearsals.'

'Actually, it's not bad,' said Jane. 'I know! I'm as surprised as you.' She said that they're all really focused on the play and it's really intense. 'It's like we're so busy they've forgotten how to be annoying,' she said. 'And Bernard the Fairy-tale Prince is a good influence. Seriously! Whenever Vanessa starts demanding stuff he kind of calms her down.' She said that Gemma, Alfie and Josh, the other members of the group, just won't put up with any nonsense from Vanessa. Or indeed Karen.

'I know it's really hard to believe,' she said. 'But we're working really well together. We've all come up with lots of good ideas for the play we have to do.'

Their play sounds very ambitious – lots of physical stuff going on. I didn't realise they were all so good at gymnastics. And I'm not sure how they're going to do the bit with the dragon, but Jane said they'll work something out.

Speaking of all things theatrical, my parents are getting even more annoying as the musical approaches. This evening I was trying to listen to music and read after my hard day's work in the world of rock, but I couldn't concentrate because they were in the kitchen singing 'Oom-pah-pah, oom-pah-pah' at top volume. And when I went in to complain and ask them to sing more quietly, they just laughed.

'I didn't think you minded a bit of noise around the house!' said Dad. 'What about your drums? You're always banging away on that little snare drum.'

'That's different,' I said. 'I'm learning an instrument! That's like homework.'

'But we're doing our homework too,' said Mum. 'And our instruments are our voices. Oom-pah-pah!' And then she and Dad laughed like fools. Sometimes I think they are not very mature for their (very) advanced age.

My fringe hasn't improved, by the way. I bumped into Mrs Mulligan and her horrible child on my way home today, and that little brat said 'Nice hair!' in a really fake voice. And then she smirked at me! It was bad enough when she was just gyrating at me. I can't believe she's moved on to actual words. I just smirked back at her and said, 'Thanks!' as her mother smiled at her and said, 'Aw, that's very nice of you Sorcha.' Clearly the little monster has fooled her poor parents into thinking she is a normal human being.

But, on the plus side, my fringe doesn't seem to have actually got worse. So that's something. And in more good news, Cass came out to Richard and Ellie and Jane. This afternoon, she asked me and Alice had we told anyone about her coming out to us. Which we hadn't. Not that her gayness is some big dark secret or anything, but we figured it was her choice to tell people or not and we shouldn't go around talking about it without telling her. After all, coming out even to her best friends was a big deal for Cass. So we told her we hadn't said anything.

'I didn't think you would have, but I thought I'd check,' said Cass. 'Anyway, I just thought I should say it was fine if you want to mention it to Richard. And I'll tell Ellie and Jane.'

So they all know now. They were all cool about it, though Richard did tell Alice later that he was a bit surprised.

'I mean, I'd never have guessed,' he said. 'She's pretty girly. She doesn't look like ... you know.'

'Like what?' said Alice fiercely.

'Ah,' said Richard. He seemed to realise how stupid he sounded. And if he didn't, he certainly did by the time Alice had given him a lecture about stereotypes and judging people by appearances and how Cass could be as girly or not-girly as she liked. But he seems to be totally fine about the whole thing anyway. As were Ellie and Jane.

'I spend half my life surrounded with my mum's hippie friends from her various goddess groups,' said Ellie. 'Gayness does not scare me.'

So Cass is relieved. It did make me realise how unfair it is that I never had to worry about people being weird about whoever I fancied. I mean, I didn't have to worry that the world would have a problem with me going out with John Kowalski, even though he was a fool. And yet Cass has to worry about people being horrible about her and Liz, who is lovely! Truly this world is an unfair place.

THURSDAY ◎

I hate that horrible Charlie! And his friends, too, though he's definitely the worst of them. We were divided into two groups for workshops this afternoon, and as soon as we walked in we realised we were in the same one as the Crack Parrots.

'Oh brilliant,' said Cass, gloomily. 'That's all we need when we try to figure out sound levels. Charlie and his goons making not-so-smart remarks.'

'Maybe they won't be so bad,' said Alice. 'I mean, surely they're not going to say anything with the mentors around.'

But it turns out that Charlie is cleverer than he looks (which wouldn't be hard, because he looks like a cocky idiot). He never said anything obnoxious when the mentors could hear. But as soon as their backs were turned or they were busy helping someone else, he'd be off.

'Are you sure you can figure out those leads?' he said, when Cass and Alice were hooking things up to the mixing-desk. 'I know girls aren't great at technical stuff ...'

'We're fine,' said Alice primly. And then she played a giant power chord on her guitar.

'Excellent, Alice,' called Kitty. 'Lovely crisp sound. Now, check your keyboard level, Cass.'

Cass played a thunderous bassline on her keyboard. It was far too loud and distorted.

'Oops,' she said.

Charlie laughed.

'I told you,' he said. 'Why don't you go and make me a sandwich instead?'

'Yeah,' said one of his bandmates, whose name is Robbie. 'We all know a girl's place is in the kitchen! Not at the mixing-desk.'

'Seriously, what did that sound like?' said Finn, the drummer.

But before we could say anything, Kitty and Dave came over.

'Everything okay?' said Kitty. 'You just need to adjust the levels there, Cass.'

'I can do it for her,' said Evan, the Crack Parrots' bass player. 'I'm pretty good at this sort of thing.'

'It's fine,' said Cass coldly. 'I've got it.' And she fiddled around with the dials and played a few notes until the keyboard sounded okay.

It was very annoying, because the class was really useful, all about how to make sure your instruments and vocals sound good together on stage. But those stupid boys put us in a bad mood. It was particularly irritating because they weren't very good at mixing their sound either, but they didn't seem to care. They still thought they were brilliant. We were all meant to be taking turns, and Charlie and Evan kept hogging the microphones for ages. Their music is rubbish too.

We cheered up a bit later, though, when Paula Howard turned out to be better than anyone else at realising what lead went where and making music sound good. Charlie looked as sick as a pig when the mentors praised her skills. But we didn't get to hear any of her music. She said she didn't want to play live yet. So she just engineered Positive Trigger for a bit. Their songs are pretty good, all about life on the mean streets and how hard it is for them to hustle their way through every day. I was quite surprised to find out that they are all actually from Clontarf, which is not very mean at all. Paperboy was from Clontarf, and his house was much bigger than mine and was also just down the road from a few posh restaurants and a supermarket my mother will only visit on special occasions because it sells nothing but fancy hummous and organic rashers. Also, two members of Positive Trigger, Oisín and Archie, go to a private school in town. But maybe Clontarf is tougher than it looks?

There was another band called Puce, who, despite their colourful name, are quite boring. Not in an obnoxious way, just in a sort of wishy-washy generic indie way. I mean, you barely noticed when they were on stage. They all look really alike too. They do have nice cardigans, but that is the only thing that sticks in the mind. And even the cardigans all look the same, so that doesn't help much. But perhaps the camp will improve their stage presence.

Anyway, I was quite sorry when the session was over, because it was all very interesting (even with poor old Puce). We were giving out about Charlie and his gang when we bumped into the art people on our way to the canteen.

'Sam,' said Alice. 'You know Charlie and Evan and all of them from school, right? Are they always really obnoxious?' She paused and looked a bit guilty. 'Um, I hope they're not your best friends. Sorry if they are.'

But Sam laughed.

'They are definitely not my best friends,' he said. 'And yes, they are mostly really obnoxious. Well, actually some of them are okay when Charlie's not around.'

'Really?' I said.

'Well, I know it's probably hard to believe, but yeah,' said Sam. 'The problem is Charlie's almost always around.'

'He's not very good at sound engineering, anyway,' said Alice. 'He was the worst of the lot.'

'Yeah, Paula was in our group too, and she was the best,' said Cass. 'Small Paula, I mean, not tall Goth Paula.'

Sam laughed. 'I bet Charlie didn't like a girl doing better than him.'

The art projects all seem to be going really well. They're each working on one big project over the whole course and then they do different challenges every day.

'Mostly still comics,' said Sam. 'But different sorts. It's really good. And I'm writing stuff too, which used to be Lucy's department.'

'How are you finding drawing?' I asked Lucy.

'Oh, it's good,' said Lucy. She looked kind of vague, as usual. 'I mean, I always liked drawing, I just didn't think I was very good at it. So I left it up to Sam. '

'She's really good,' said Sam. 'I always told her she should do more of it, and she ignored me! But it looks like this course is going to succeed where I failed.'

I hope I didn't say anything to upset Lucy. She never looks me totally in the eye. I mean, she's not very friendly. I hope she doesn't think any of us are after Sam, because I'm certainly not. And neither is Ellie, because she likes another boy on the course (his name is Cillian but it turns out he has a girlfriend and talks about her all the time so poor Ellie knows she doesn't have a chance).

Anyway, Ellie has lots of work to distract her because she is going to make the costumes for Jane and the crazy people's play. It will be her big project in the art course. She says it's quite a challenge.

'I'm not sure what I'm going to do about the dragon,' she said. 'I mean, it's not exactly a normal costume. And I have to make sure they can do gymnastics and juggling in most of the outfits. And that they'll be okay for the human pyramid bit. But I'll figure something out.'

Speaking of stage ensembles, my parents went off to collect their costumes for their own musical this evening. A member of the musical society is making most of them, and she only lives down the road so she suggested they call round for a fitting. My dad took photos of them on his phone, and all I can say is I hope they add some fabric to Mum's outfit. I know she is meant to be some sort of Victorian floozy, but surely she doesn't need to show so much chest? It's a bit much, especially at her age. I mentioned to her that it was a bit low-cut, and she just LAUGHED.

'Come on, Bex, it's hardly indecent exposure!' she said. 'Would you prefer all women over the age of thirty-five go around wearing sacks?'

'Of course not!' I said. 'I'm just worried you'll ... feel self-conscious.'

But she just rolled her eyes and told me to chop some leeks. She clearly doesn't appreciate my concern. As usual. I don't know why I bother.

FRIDAY ☺

Today we had a workshop in stage performance. The mentor who was doing it is called Shane O'Driscoll. He is the lead singer of a band called The Invited, who aren't my sort of thing, but lots of girls really fancy him for some reason. He is definitely not my type, though. He is kind of hunky in a fairy-tale prince sort of way, and his hair is all tousled with gel. He has lots of tattoos in Chinese lettering, and he wears leather trousers and lots of leather wristlets and necklaces and things. Which must be very hot in this weather, now I come to think of it. I was wearing a denim skirt with bare legs today, and I was still roasting.

Shane believes it's really important for bands to put on a big show. He started off by saying that we all have to find our own way to capture the crowd's attention, but I think he thought his own way was the best.

'You've really got to put your soul into your performance,' he said, which is fair enough. But then he said, 'I like to gesture to the crowd, like I'm singing straight to their hearts. And when I reach a particularly emotional part of the song, I like to stretch out one hand and then draw it back to my chest, like I'm pulling the audience closer.'

I tried to imagine me and Cass and Alice doing that on stage. I couldn't, not least because we're all playing instruments most of the time. If I started waving my arms around and opening and clenching my fists, I'd drop my drumsticks.

'I also have a move I call "prowling",' said Shane. 'I like to walk from one side of the stage to the other like a panther, looking out at the audience the entire time. It's like I become a charismatic big cat.'

I can't imagine Alice prowling across the stage like a panther. Or any sort of charismatic big cat. She's the only one of us who could even try, because me and Cass are stuck behind instruments. If we tried prowling we'd have to push our instruments in front of us as we went around the stage, which wouldn't look very cool.

Shane also suggested that we think about having stage sets, which, of course, was music to Cass's ears.

'When Bon Jovi toured a few years ago they had a big set that looked like a scuzzy nightclub,' said Shane. 'Loads of neon signs, poles, that sort of thing. You could build some props, create a proper stage set.'

I could tell that Cass was getting quite excited at the thought. I looked at her.

'No, Cass,' I whispered. 'You are not making us a scuzzy nightclub. Anyway, you don't even know how to make neon signs.'

'I don't want to,' she said. 'But we could do something else.'

She could be on to something, I suppose. Maybe we could have some sort of set. Maybe we could make the stage look like, I dunno, an ordinary sitting room. Or even the shed where we practise. But definitely no neon. Or poles.

Anyway, Cass wasn't the only one who was intrigued by Shane. Niall, the lead singer of Puce, looked like he was listening very intently all the way through, even when Shane was praising his own leather trousers.

'These old trews are a part of me now,' said Shane, which didn't sound like a good thing to me. 'They're like my rock uniform. The way I see it, if you want to be a rock god, you've got to dress like a rock god! So find your uniform. It could be leather. It could be feathers. It could be denim. It could be eye-catching jumpsuits. It's up to you.'

I could see Niall taking notes. I can't imagine him in an eye-catching jumpsuit, but you never know, maybe he could pull it off.

Shane is also fond of explosions and fireworks and trap doors – 'Audiences love seeing you pop out of a trap door!' – but he admitted that we might find arranging all of these things quite difficult when we're only starting out.

Anyway, it was all quite interesting, especially when we got the chance to try out some of the techniques (sadly we didn't get to try out trapdoors or fireworks. Or, indeed, jumpsuits). Tall Paula from Exquisite Corpse was particularly good at prowling. She even did a bit of a panther-esque snarl as she paced from one side of the stage to the other, which made Shane nod seriously and say, 'Very good, Paula. You've got great stage presence.' Small Paula, however, didn't want to perform at all.

'Don't you want to give it a try?' asked Alice. But Small Paula shook her head.

'Not yet,' she said. 'I'm not ready.'

'Fair enough,' said Alice, but we were all a bit disappointed. Now Small Paula is the only person on the course whose music we haven't heard yet. It is very intriguing. I can actually imagine her prowling like a panther, even though she looks more like a small pony than a big cat, with that impressive fringe.

LATER

I just tried doing some prowling in front of my mirror, but I'm not sure I pulled it off. I think I looked a bit silly. Also, whenever I looked in the mirror, I couldn't help noticing my stupid fringe, which was starting to work its way out of its hairpins and fall down over my face. Of course, it didn't help that I turned around and saw that horrible Mulligan brat across the road laughing her hideous head off at me. I just glared at her and drew the curtains. I can't believe that appalling child is forcing me to live in darkness in the middle of summer just because she has no manners.

SATURDAY ☺

Today we had the first proper Hey Dollface sweet-making session because Alice was FINALLY free at the weekend. So we all went round to Cass's house to work our magic. We had plenty to talk about before we started our sweet-making because Cass came out to her parents last night. She hadn't even planned it. Apparently her little brother Nick was being really annoying at the dinner table and going on about the summer camp and asking whether Cass had fallen in LUUURVE (as he put it) with any of the boys on it. He just wouldn't shut up so eventually Cass got really annoyed and told him to go away. Except she didn't actually say 'go away'.

And her mother gave out to her for using a rude word and to Nick for trying to annoy her, but afterwards, when Nick had gone off to do whatever stupid twelve-year-old-boy stuff he does, her mum got all serious and said that she wasn't to ever worry about not having a boyfriend, and the thought of her mother having a 'serious chat' about LOVE with her was so horrible that Cass said, 'I'm not worried, I'm gay!' basically just to shut her up.

Anyway, not only was Brenda (for that is Cass's mother's name, and she insists that we are on first-name terms) not upset, but she reacted a bit TOO well. She seems to think that having a lesbian daughter makes her cool ('As if anything could,' said Cass), and she keeps going on about it and trying to be all understanding. Like, 'Well, Cass, as a lesbian, I'm sure you appreciate this ...' Cass says it is terrible, and I can see why. In fact, Cass is starting to wish she'd never told her at all. But, as she said herself, 'Her being so freakishly positive about it is much better than the other way around.'

She much preferred her dad's reaction, though. He was a bit surprised, and then he said, 'And do you really like this girl?' And Cass said yes. And he gave her a hug and said, 'Well, if you're happy then I'm happy, Boldness.' And Cass was so touched she didn't even mind him calling her Boldness, which was her family nickname when she was very very small and which usually drives her mad if her parents call her it. So it has worked out very well.

Anyway, Brenda only told us how great it is to be gay once while we were making our fudge, and then she went off to her Pilates class. Our fudge went really well. I think we're getting the hang of it at last, although maybe it was better than our previous efforts because this time there were three of us so we could share out the beating of the ingredients. It was much less exhausting than when it was just me and Cass. We also put on music so we could work in time to our favourite tracks.

It was still surprisingly hard work, even with Alice and the music, but it paid off. Even Nick, who is the sort of rude person who just spits out any food he doesn't like, said it was 'not bad'. Which is high praise coming from him.

'Maybe we could experiment next time,' I said. 'Like, add nuts. Or chocolate. Or a different flavouring. Like, I dunno, orange or lemon or something.'

'Or raisins,' said Cass.

'Ugh, no, I hate raisins,' I said. 'What do you think, Alice?'

'Hmm, I don't know,' said Alice. 'Maybe we should perfect the vanilla sort first.'

'I think it's perfect already!' said Cass, and we did a special triumphal dance around the kitchen, which Alice eventually joined in.

Poor Cass is missing Liz, though. Even our dancing (and our delicious creations) weren't enough to make her forget her sorrow for the whole afternoon. Liz's phone was confiscated at the Irish college, and she has only been able to ring Cass once when she was meant to be ringing her parents. In their very brief conversation, she told Cass that when they arrived it was like one of those films where someone goes to prison and has to hand over all their possessions. And then they get them back, like, ten years later and everything's out of date. Anyway, it sounds pretty tough, though apparently the actual Irish college is quite fun apart from the lack of phones and internet access, and she has learned how to do lots of set dances. Not that this is any consolation for poor Cass.

'I feel like she's been gone forever,' said Cass. 'And it's only been two weeks!'

I know how she feels, of course. I too have known the anguish of long-distance love. Although a part of me thinks

Cass is making a fuss out of not very much. I mean, Liz will be back in two weeks. Paperboy went to Canada forever! That is true misery. But I didn't say that to Cass. I don't think it would have cheered her up.

It did all remind me, yet again, of my lonely single state. I had such a fun afternoon, but when I got home I felt a bit sad. I don't even know why I feel so bad. It's not like the others would make me feel left out. It's just that I can't help feeling I'll never meet anyone again. I mean, like I said before, I am surrounded by boys at the camp, and I still don't fancy any of them. And it's not like I fancy any of the girls either. I've wondered about whether I ever could, especially since Cass came out, but I haven't so far. Though surely any girl would be preferable to, say, Charlie. Except, you know, Vanessa or someone. Anyway, I don't fancy any girls or boys on the camp. And I know it shouldn't be a big deal. But when I think about Cass and Alice being all loved up, it feels like it is. And then I feel guilty for feeling bad about my friends being happy. Life is very complicated sometimes.

SUNDAY ☼

To distract myself from my own self-pity, I have done some more work on those song lyrics about John Kowalski. It is still quite tricky. I tried putting in 'I met you at a musical' instead of 'rehearsal' but not much rhymes with 'musical' either. Still, I gave it a try.

> *I met you at a musical*
> *You got there on a bicycle*

Though that doesn't totally work either. Also, he didn't get there on a bicycle. I don't know if he even owned one. The only time I ever saw him near any bikes was when he was smoking by the bike racks.

LATER

Oh my God, I have found the most amazing thing ever to help me in my song writing! It is a rhyming dictionary, and you can look up any word and see what rhymes with it. I can't believe it was in my house all the time and I didn't know about it. I took a break after writing that last bit about John and went down to get a glass of juice. And when I was there I happened to mention to my mum that it was hard finding words to rhyme when we were writing songs.

'Why don't you use a rhyming dictionary?' she said. 'I'm sure I've got one somewhere in my study.'

And she did! And it is like magic! There are loads of words that rhyme with 'musical' that I never even thought of! In fact, I have never even heard of lots of them. Like 'caulicle', which is apparently a 'small plant stalk'. Not that I can compare John to a small plant stalk. But it just shows how many interesting words are out there. There is also 'ossicle', which is a bone in the ear. Of course, I can't use that either. But there are so many words on the list I must be able to use some of them. There are loads of words that rhyme with 'rehearsal' too. It's brilliant.

LATER

I think I have the perfect rhyme!

I met him at rehearsal
He looked just like a tercel

A tercel is a 'male falcon or hawk'. I didn't know that until I saw it the rhyming dictionary. But actually, it describes John Kowalski well because there is something haughty and bird-of-prey-esque about him. This book's brilliant. I don't know how I ever wrote songs without it! I am going to go and write some more lyrics now.

MONDAY ☀

Today we realised we have actually started calling Small Paula 'Small Paula', like it's her actual name. A bunch of us were sitting around having lunch after our excellent morning's workshop with Kitty when Alice opened a packet of sweets and offered them to everyone. Paula was sitting at the far end of the table, and Alice waved the packet in her direction.

'Do you want one, Small Paula?' she said, in a friendly way. Then she looked horrified when she realised what she'd said.

Small Paula looked a bit surprised, then she said, 'Yes please', and took one.

'Alice!' said Cass. 'You can't call Paula Small Paula!'

'Oh dear,' said Alice miserably. 'Sorry, Paula.'

'But it's not meant in a mean way. It's a nice name,' I said. 'And it's just to distinguish Sma... that Paula from the other Paula. Um, Tall Paula, from Exquisite Corpse.'

'That's as may be,' said Cass, sounding like a wise old lady, 'but it's not up to us to decide whether what we call other people is nice or not. It's up to them. I might think calling you ... I dunno, Small-ish Rebecca is nice, but you still might find it really annoying.'

'That's true, I suppose,' I admitted. 'You don't ever call me that, do you?'

'No,' said Cass. 'Not yet, anyway.'

'Do you mind being called Small Paula, Paula?' said Alice. 'I'm very sorry.'

'No,' said Small Paula from beneath her fringe. 'I like it.'

'Fair enough,' said Cass.

'It's quite a good stage name, actually,' I said. 'What do you think, Paula?'

But Small Paula clearly felt she'd talked enough for one day, so she just nodded her fringe at us in a friendly fashion (it was like a small pony shaking its mane) and scuttled off carrying her giant box of leads.

'Bye, Small Paula,' said Cass.

'I wonder what sort of music she's making?' I said. 'I bet it's all ethereal and mysterious.'

'I bet it's sort of folky,' said Cass. 'Maybe with some electronic beats.'

'I wonder will we ever get to find out?' I said. 'I mean, it's not like doing a gig is compulsory.'

'I think Small Paula might be just making music for herself,' said Alice. 'Which adds to her mystery.'

And we all thought for a minute about what an enigma Small Paula is. I wish I was a bit more enigmatic. I asked Cass and Alice if I was mysterious at all, and they laughed and laughed. When they'd recovered, Alice said, 'Maybe if someone didn't know you they might think you were mysterious.'

'That doesn't count!' I said. 'Everyone's mysterious if you don't know them. I want people who do know me to wonder what I'm thinking.'

'You generally show what you're thinking,' said Cass. 'It's usually pretty obvious.'

'No it isn't!' I said.

'Yes it is,' said Cass. 'I mean, you're feeling quite cross

right now, aren't you?'

Gah, she was right. I am going to try and be more mysterious. After all, most of the people here don't know me very well. I bet I can cultivate an air of mystery if I try.

TUESDAY ☾

I am not sure my plan to cultivate an air of mystery is going very well. I ended up chatting to Sam for a while at lunch today, and at first I thought it was a good opportunity to try being all enigmatic.

'So,' said Sam, 'how is it going with your mentor? Richard was saying his guy is great.'

'Ah yes,' I said. 'Ian Cliff.' Then I paused in what I hoped was an enigmatic sort of way. Sam looked at me in an expectant fashion.

'What about him?' he said.

'Oh,' I said. 'Um, just that he's Richard's mentor. Ours is ... well, she's beyond words, really. I mean, you can't describe her.' And I looked into the distance, mysteriously.

'Yes, that's usually what beyond words means,' said Sam,

which could have sounded like a dig but didn't. 'Are you okay?'

'I'm fine,' I said. And then I couldn't think of anything mysterious to say. It seems that there is a very fine line between being mysterious and being, well, a bit rude and unfriendly. And it turns out I am more worried about being rude than about being mysterious, so I said, 'So, how are the comics going?' in a normal voice.

'Really good,' said Sam. 'The facilitator is great. Yesterday she told us to bring in a book we've always loved, and today we had to, like, adapt a page or a scene from it in comic form.'

'Wow, that's a cool idea!' I said. 'What book did you bring in?'

Sam looked a bit embarrassed. 'Um, you probably haven't read it,' he said. 'It's called *My Family and Other Animals*, it's a true story about a boy who moves to a Greek island and has loads of animals ...'

'By Gerald Durrell! I love that book!' I said.

Sam looked surprised. 'Seriously?'

'Yeah, of course!' I said. 'It's really funny, and I like the animal stuff. Also, I share the hero's pain because he has very annoying siblings, and I have a very annoying big sister.'

'Heh, so do I,' said Sam. 'She's even worse than Gerald's

brother Larry. I love the bit when ...' And we talked about our favourite bits of the book for a while. It wasn't like talking about books with John Kowalski. John was very good at talking passionately about something he loved, and it was sometimes very exciting, but now I have to admit that it was more like being at a lecture than, like, having a conversation. Talking to Sam was much more ordinary – we kept interrupting each other and laughing. It wasn't intense and exciting, like with John. It was fun though.

'So what other authors do you really like?' said Sam.

'Oh God, too many to list,' I said. But I mentioned a few of my favourites, like Nancy Mitford and Rachel Caine's vampire books. I have very broad tastes, if I say so myself.

'Have you ever read *Sandman*?' said Sam. 'It's a graphic novel series, and it's really great. A bit scary, but brilliant.'

'How scary?' I said. 'I like fantasy stuff, but nothing too, like, gross or disturbing. And I don't like stuff where all the characters are, you know, elves and stuff. I like books where magic stuff happens to realistic people.'

'Um, it's medium scary,' said Sam. 'And it's set in our world, mostly. The guy who wrote it also wrote *Coraline*, the kids' book. Have you read that?'

'Ooh, yes!' I said. 'I loved it. It was creepy though. But in a good way.'

'He did a book with Terry Pratchett called *Good Omens* which is brilliant too,' said Sam. 'Kind of scary, but mostly funny. I can lend it to you if you like.'

'Yes, please,' I said. And then the bell rang for the afternoon workshops.

'See you later,' said Sam. 'And I'll bring in *Good Omens* tomorrow!'

'Cool, thanks!' I said, and then I realised I was on the other side of the building to the Orchestra Room, so I had to run off. It wasn't until I was sitting there in a big circle with all the other bands listening to Eli Gavroche, Positive Trigger's mentor, talk to us about mixing tracks that I realised I had ended up not being very mysterious at all. I have a horrible feeling you're either enigmatic or you're not. And I'm probably not.

It was nice talking to Sam, though. He has very good taste in books. I sort of wish I fancied him, but I don't really think I do. It's not that he's ugly, it's just that ... I dunno. There is no magic spark there like there was with Paperboy. Or even John Kowalski. Actually, with John it was basically all spark and nothing else. But just a bit of spark with someone would be good.

Oh no, my parents are back from their *Oliver!* rehearsal. I can hear them singing 'Who Will Buy This Wonderful Morning?' I certainly won't. Why is this house always so noisy? There's no peace around here! I will practise my drumming to drown out their caterwauling. Good thing I brought my snare drum home from our last band practice.

WEDNESDAY ✿

Everyone is better at being mysterious than me! Cass was acting a bit oddly this afternoon. She said she wouldn't be walking home with us because she had to go into town, but when I asked why, she got all cagey.

'It's no big deal,' she said. 'I just have something to do.' And she sounded so awkward I just left it. But what can it be? Surely if it was something to do with her family she'd tell us. And she didn't seem really upset or anything. It can't be anything romantic because she certainly hasn't forgotten about Liz. Unless she has decided to run away to visit Liz in Connemara. Although I can't imagine how she'd get down there. She only has about five euro until Saturday, and that wouldn't get her very far by public transport. And how else could she get there? I know she really likes Liz and everything, but I can't imagine she'd actually walk all the way across the country to see her.

Anyway, Small Paula is definitely more mysterious than all of us. We still have no idea what her music sounds like. Today we had a recording workshop led by Dave, Paula's mentor, who was very good. We are all going to get some studio time over the next week or so to try and record a few tracks, which is cool. Paula was in the workshop too, but she didn't really need to be there because, as Dave mentioned, she has already recorded quite a bit of stuff on her computer at home. She is a technical master.

'Can we hear some of your stuff, Paula?' asked Cass.

'Sorry, but no,' said Small Paula, shaking her fringe firmly. 'It's all top secret.'

'Just one song?' said Alice hopefully.

'All will be revealed,' said Paula, and then she scuttled off. So now we are even more intrigued.

Speaking of secret songwriting, I think I have completed my lyrics for the song about John. I told the others I was working on some words and I'd show them when I was ready, so I will reveal all tomorrow. I wonder if anyone will be able to tell that

I got lots of words from my rhyming dictionary? I really think it has enhanced my writing, because I'd never have thought of using lots of these words if I hadn't seen them in the book. Anyway, here are the lyrics:

I met you at rehearsal
You looked just like a tercel
Oh-oh, oh-oh
You went out for a smoke break
And I felt my heart quake
Oh-oh, oh-oh

CHORUS
But now it's hard to know
What I ever saw in you
And when I think about you
I feel like I have the flu
It makes me want to run away
To Machu Picchu

We walked down Griffith Avenue
We didn't have a retinue

Oh-oh, oh-oh

Kissing at the corner

Not feeling like a mourner

Oh-oh, oh-oh

CHORUS

But now it's hard to know

What I ever saw in you

And when I think about you

I feel like I have the flu

It makes me want to run away

To Machu Picchu

Then I saw you were a snob

My heart it did not throb

Oh-oh, oh-oh

You left us in the lurch

Our show's name you did besmirch

Oh-oh, oh-oh

CHORUS

But now it's hard to know

What I ever saw in you
And when I think about you
I feel like I have the flu
It makes me want to run away
To Machu Picchu

REPEAT CHORUS ONCE MORE.

I am pretty pleased with it, though there were a few problems even with the rhyming dictionary. Not many words rhyme with 'avenue', for example. In fact, I'm not totally sure that 'retinue' does rhyme with it, even though it was on the list in the dictionary. And it was particularly tricky finding a match for 'corner' because the dictionary is British and assumes you have the sort of English accent that makes 'corner' rhyme with 'sauna' and 'fauna'. In fact, 'mourner' was the only word on that list that would work for Dublin people. But I think it goes in the song quite well.

Anyway, I will show it to the others tomorrow. I bet they'll be impressed at how my songwriting has developed. Unless, of course, Cass really has run away (literally, considering her financial situation) to Connemara. But she probably hasn't.

THURSDAY ◎

The mystery of Cass's behaviour has been revealed! When I met her this morning, there was definitely something different about her.

'Why are you staring at me?' said Cass nervously.

'No reason,' I said. Then it struck me. 'Aha!' I said.

'What?' said Cass.

'You got your hair cut!' I said. 'Was that where you were going yesterday?'

'Um, yeah,' said Cass, guiltily. 'I needed to get my fringe cut. But I didn't want to mention that I was going in to see Cliona in case it brought back terrible memories of your fringe experience.'

Cass can be surprisingly thoughtful sometimes. Of course I told her she didn't have to feel bad about going back to Cliona.

'I mean, she does a very good job on your fringe,' I said. 'I think it's more my hair's fault than hers. And I think I've mastered the whole pinning it back thing.'

'It looks pretty good,' said Cass. 'You can't even see all the pins from the front.'

Cass is truly a noble friend. And she is rocking her newly

shorn look. Ever since she has embraced the fringe her hair has looked great (unlike me. But I don't want to think about my fringe today).

And we are not the only people on the course to embrace different styles. Niall from Puce seems to have taken Shane O'Driscoll's advice to heart. He appeared at today's songwriting workshop wearing a big leather biker jacket and some biker boots. It was quite a contrast to his usual cardigan and desert boots. It's not my sort of look, but he definitely looked a bit tougher than usual when he wearing it, like a bad boy from an American soap opera.

Of course, Charlie and his gang thought Niall looked hilarious because if anyone does anything new or different they think it's stupid. They were sitting in front of us, and when Niall came in, Charlie said, 'God, look at Puke boy!' That is his hilarious name for Niall. (Because of his band being called Puce. Yes, that's how sophisticated Charlie's sense of humour is.) 'I didn't think he could look any more gay until I saw him in that leather,' Charlie went on. Finn, the band's drummer, was sitting next to him, and he laughed so much he choked on the Coke he was drinking.

Luckily, Niall was on the other side of the room for the

workshop so I don't think he heard them. In fact, I have noticed that Charlie tends not to say anything to other boys' faces. Maybe he's afraid one of them will hit him. Obviously I don't approve of violence, but I sort of wish someone would, male or female. Actually, preferably female. He'd think that was worse.

But there are plenty of nice boys around too, even if some of them are going a bit mad. Richard is becoming more and more Ian Cliff-esque. His hair has gradually been moving upwards until today he had what can only be described as a quiff. And I bet he'd be wearing that posh suit of his brother's every day if he could manage to steal it (apparently his brother started hiding it after he discovered Richard had stolen it for the Battle of the Bands last year). As he has no suit, he has just started wearing very fitted, quite formal shirts and alarmingly tight trousers in an effort to look taller. He is actually quite tall already, but Ian Cliff is practically a giant. I don't think there's anything else Richard can do to copy that unless he starts wearing platform shoes. But despite his Ian Cliff worship, he really is sound. I'm glad Alice is going out with someone I actually get on with.

And, of course, Richard isn't the only decent boy around

here. Jane has become friendly with a boy called Jamie who is doing the drama class. He is a bit older than us but he's very nice. He wants to do drama when he goes to college next year, which immediately reminded me of John Kowalski, but he talked about it in a much less dramatic way than John did. Though of course that wouldn't be hard. Jamie talks about studying drama the same way someone might talk about doing English or computer science or any other subject, whereas John talked about it like he was on a mission from God.

And Sam brought in that *Good Omens* book for me today (he forgot it yesterday).

'If you like funny fantasy stuff you'll definitely like this,' he said. 'I hope. Let me know what you think, anyway.'

He is so nice, like the Anti-Charlie. I'm still not sure about Lucy, though. I passed her in the foyer today, and she just looked past me like I didn't exist. Could it actually be because she thinks I'm after Sam, what with all the book-lending stuff, and she's jealous? Not that I've got the impression there's anything going on between them. Maybe she just doesn't like me?

Speaking of not liking people, I had managed to forget all about the Mrs-Harrington-being-in-Mum's-book thing, but I was reminded of it this evening. Mum was in an unusually good mood, marching around the house singing songs from *Oliver!*. It turns out she'd sent the first few chapters of her book to her editor, and her editor really liked it.

'And her favourite character is Patricia Alexandra!' she said. 'She said she's my greatest villain yet.'

'Are you sure you wouldn't like to ... I dunno, give her a softer side?' I said. 'I mean, maybe she could see the light at the end and become good and save the heroine's bakery.'

I genuinely thought this was pretty clever of me. I mean, surely this would make Patricia Alexandra Harrington more complex and interesting? But Mum just laughed at my brilliant idea.

'Sorry, Rebecca,' she said. 'But the character is working the way she is. And she's going to get her comeuppance at the end!'

Oh dear. I don't know what to do. If I keep going on about this, she's going to get suspicious that something's up. After all, I don't usually show so much interest in her books.

But I should be able to come up with something. Shouldn't I? I mean, my mother is not the only creative person in the family. I shared my lyrics with Cass and Alice today, and they went down pretty well, even if they did question some of my innovative word choices.

'It's a really good idea for a song,' said Cass. 'And I particularly like the chorus. But what is a tercel?'

'It's a male falcon or hawk,' I said.

'Oh,' said Cass. She looked thoughtful. 'Hmmm. I suppose John does look a bit like one.'

'Exactly!' I said.

So we are sticking with my lyrics. They really do go well with the song, if I say so myself. In fact, I can't wait to get out my trusty rhyming dictionary and write some more words to the song we started working on this morning with Kitty. She is great at offering suggestions without, like, imposing her own ideas on us.

I love working with her so much. We've written a few songs over the last week and a half (even though most of them don't have words yet), and we'd never have done all that without her encouragement. She is really nice, and her band are very good. They're actually playing a gig tomorrow night. I wish we could go, but it's in a pub so our parents would never let us. And, to be honest, we wouldn't get in even if they did. Even when we're all dressed up and wearing make-up I don't think we could pass for older than sixteen at the very, very most.

And that would be pushing it. Rachel says we all look about twelve, though of course she is exaggerating (and it's not like she even looks her age either). My mum always says we'll be glad of our youthful looks when we're thirty, but that's not much comfort now.

FRIDAY ☺

I really don't know how Jane is managing to put up with Vanessa. I know she says Vanessa is different when they're actually working on their play, but unless she has a complete personality transplant every time she enters the rehearsal room, I can't understand how anyone can bear her. And Karen's almost as bad. Today a gang of us were having some Cokes during the morning break, and Vanessa, Karen and Bernard the Fairy-tale Prince sat down at the other end of the table. Which is how we couldn't help overhearing Vanessa talking about her new insane plans.

'I'm going to invite some agents to see our showcase,' she was saying.

'You mean the play?' said Bernard. 'Oh Vanessa, I don't

know if that's a good idea.'

'Of course it's a good idea!' said Karen.

'I can't believe this camp isn't inviting agents anyway,' sniffed Vanessa. 'They're so unprofessional here.'

'Well, it is meant to be a camp for amateurs,' said Bernard. But this didn't go down well.

'Bernard, I'm surprised at you!' said Karen. 'We can't think of ourselves as mere amateurs.'

'Karen's so right,' said Vanessa. 'We need to think of ourselves as stars! I, of course, already do.'

Good grief. I am starting to feel very sorry for Bernard the Fairy-tale Prince. He seems relatively sane in comparison to his awful girlfriend and Vanessa.

Then Vanessa noticed us at the end of the table.

'You must agree with me, Bert,' she said to Richard.

'It's Richard,' said Richard. 'And I can't say I do. We're not pros yet. We're here to, like, gain experience and learn stuff from the experts.'

Vanessa just tossed her hair crossly and turned away.

'God,' she said. 'Karen, we really are the only professionals in this place.'

If by 'professionals' she means 'deluded fools', then I suppose she's right. But at least she's not as bad as that horrible Charlie. Alice and I had another run-in with him and his goons. It was actually really disgusting. The two of us were on our way back from the loo at lunch. We going down a corridor in the arts building when we passed the Crack Parrots, looking at something on Finn the drummer's mobile and laughing. As soon as we got near to them, Charlie went, 'Hey, girls, what do you think of this?' And when he held up the phone there was a porn video playing on it. I looked away quickly so I didn't see any details, but it was obvious what it was. It made me feel a bit sick and sort of upset. I couldn't even think of anything to say. But Alice just glared at him and said, 'Oh, you're into sexual harassment now?' and marched me along the corridor. She is always very good in a crisis. She never loses her head. Evan looked a bit uncomfortable, but the others just laughed more. They're such revolting pigs. And Evan didn't say anything to them so he can't have minded that much.

Anyway, when we got back to the canteen, we told Cass, Jane and her drama mate Gemma what had happened. Gemma said she'd seen the Crack Parrots looking at porn a few days ago.

'They don't even care who sees them,' she said. 'They have no shame.'

Luckily we had a workshop with Kitty in the afternoon so we didn't have to see the Crack Parrots again today. It was a really good workshop too, all about performing on stage, and it was actually more useful than Shane O'Driscoll's more dramatic workshop last week. Kitty isn't into big gestures and prowling. She says that her key to looking confident is to just put your head back and chin up and kind of stare down at the audience. I will definitely give this a try when we play next week. Practising my haughty stare was a lot of fun and made me forget about the Crack Parrots for a while. But now I almost wish I'd said something to Kitty about what they did. I mean, surely they can't be allowed to go around showing random girls stuff like that?

Ugh. I don't want to think about them now. I will go and read that book Sam lent me instead. It is very good. Actually, it features a boy who is the spawn of Satan. So maybe it will not be much of a distraction from Charlie after all.

SATURDAY ☺

More sweet-making practice today! This time we were back in

my house, which meant that we had to put up with the sound of my parents singing songs from *Oliver!* all afternoon. Clearly all those years of yelling at her long-suffering daughters have taught Mum how to project her voice because you could hear her bellowing all over the house.

'Sorry about this,' I said, as the strains of 'Pick a Pocket or Two' echoed around the kitchen. 'I thought they were going on one of their boring trips to the garden centre today. But they've gone musical mad.'

'I actually quite like it,' said Alice. 'I mean, they can actually sing.'

'What?!' I said. 'Alice, are you sure all the loud music of the last few weeks hasn't damaged your ears?' But she insisted she found the sound of my mum crooning 'Who Will Buy This Wonderful Morning?' at top volume delightful. I don't know what's come over her. At least Cass had an excuse for tolerating my parental warbling (though she wasn't quite as enthusiastic about it as Alice). She's in a very good mood because Liz is coming home on Monday.

'We only got together about five minutes before she went off to Connemara!' she said. 'It's so unfair. Well, you know what that's like,' she added to me.

'I do,' I said. Though I didn't add that when Paperboy left I knew he wasn't coming back and Cass knew Liz would be back in three weeks. That would have been a bit churlish.

Anyway, the fudge turned out pretty well (possibly because we put on loud music to drown out my parents, and then danced around to it as we stirred, which kept us full of enthusiasm). In fact, it was our best yet.

'You know,' I said. 'We could actually start selling this soon.'

'I dunno,' said Alice. 'Didn't your mum say we needed, like, a food licence or something to sell things to the general public? And I think if you sell food someone has to come and inspect your kitchen.'

'Oh yeah,' I said. 'Hmmm.' I looked around our kitchen. On the counter, next to the mixing bowl, was a big pile of magazines, a cup half full of cold tea left over from this morning and a bag of Bumpers' cat food. I don't think it would pass any official inspections.

'Well, we've got to start somewhere,' I said. 'Newspapers always have articles about people who start businesses in their kitchens. It can't be that hard.'

'We could always try building up a potential customer base,' said Cass.

'You sound very business-like, Cass,' I said. 'I'm impressed.'

'I thought you would be,' said Cass. 'Anyway, I was thinking we could give some away next week. When we do our gig at the end of the camp.'

'Wow, that's actually a good idea,' I said. 'Maybe we could even make the little boxes! With that logo you designed.'

'Yes!' said Alice. 'Though we'd have to find lots of boxes.'

We decided we could sort those details out later. After all, it's almost two weeks until the final gigs. Well, a week and a half. Then we sat around in my room and ate the fudge and talked about the camp.

'Sam's really nice, isn't he?' said Cass.

'So's Lucy,' said Alice. 'Though she's very quiet.'

'I don't think she likes me,' I said.

'Why on earth do you think that?' said Alice.

'I dunno,' I said. And I didn't really. Mostly because she doesn't say anything. Then I thought of something. 'The other day she just stared straight past me when I saw her in the foyer. And whenever I talk to her and Sam she doesn't say anything, she just looks like she's looking down on me.'

'She is looking down on you,' said Cass. 'Because she's, like, four inches taller than you. That's not her fault.'

'I think you might have a bit of a complex about tall people,' said Alice. 'I don't think you like them.'

'What?!' I said. 'That's ridiculous. Look at my family! They're all fairly tall apart from me. I take after my granny on my dad's side, but my whole family are, like, giants.'

Cass and Alice looked at each other in what I'm sure they thought was a very wise way but which was just really irritating instead.

'Exactly,' said Alice. 'That's why.'

I hate it when they think they're psychologists.

Anyway, as I told them, I don't dislike Lucy. I just think she doesn't like me. Which isn't the same thing at all.

SUNDAY ☼

It is Rachel's birthday on Thursday. She is going to be seventeen. I suppose I should get her something though I am not sure she deserves it. Her oh-so-perfect boyfriend Tom is back from his holidays, and he called over to our house this afternoon when our parents were out at the garden centre buying pots and compost and other boring things (if only they'd actually gone out yesterday when my friends were here). Rachel basically forced me out of the sitting room so she and Tom could have it to themselves. I shudder to think what they were up to, although when I said that to her she got really annoyed and said that I had a filthy mind and they just wanted some 'alone time' without me 'hovering around and annoying us'.

As if I would. I'd rather not be anywhere near them. Anyway, whatever they were up to, I can't see why they didn't just go up to her room rather than forcing me out into the back garden like some sort of dog. The only good thing was that for once I had some credit on my phone so I could ring Alice. As ever, Alice was the voice of reason and pointed out that it was a lovely day and actually it was nicer out in the garden. She is very soothing sometimes. Though she did go too far when she said she's always wished she had a sister and that I should count my blessings. Alice has always been into counting blessings, though I don't think Rachel is one. A blessing, I mean. She is more like a curse. I said this to Alice, and she reminded me that, actually, Rachel has been okay to me a few times over the last year.

'She gave you pretty good advice about Paperboy and John, didn't she?' she said. 'And she was great about helping you defeat your fringe. And she even did your make-up for the Battle of the Bands.'

This is all true. I suppose she isn't a curse all the time. I'm not sure I'd go so far as to call her a blessing, though. Anyway, maybe I will get her a present after all. Not that I have much money to splash out on lavish gifts. Maybe I will write Rachel a song instead? I know I won't have the band to play the music, but I can just sing it to her. And surely a personalised song is a gift more precious than anything you could buy in a shop. It is also much cheaper.

LATER

It is surprisingly difficult to write a song for Rachel. I mean, I'm pretty sure nothing rhymes with Rachel – there are no actual names in my dictionary, so I can't even look it up. Not that many useful words rhyme with 'sister', either. Can I compare her to a fillister? Apparently, that is a word for an 'adjustable plane', whatever that is. Or a lister, which is a sort of plough? Probably not. Anyway, this is what I have so far:

You're two years older than me
That's where you'll always be
You are my big sister
Sometimes I say you are a blister
But I don't mean it when you're nice to me

You've given me advice about boys
You do have a certain poise
And so I steal your clothes
When I'm feeling morose
And I hope you won't make a noise

So happy birthday, sister dear
And enjoy your eighteenth year
This song is your present
I hope you think it is pleasant
And that it fills you with good cheer

I'm not sure it's one of my best. It doesn't actually have a chorus. And it sort of makes it look like the only good things about Rachel are her ability to give boy advice and the fact that she has nice clothes which I can steal. Which makes her look a bit shallow and me a bit selfish. But seriously, it just took me ages to write, and I don't think I can manage any more. Anyway, it's the thought that counts. And surely just having a song written just for you is a lovely present?

LATER

Rachel went out to her friend Jenny's house so I thought I'd sing my song to Mum. She looked very thoughtful as I was singing, and when I was finished she cleared her throat and said, 'That's really good, love. And it's a really good present. But if you want to get her anything else, I'll give you some money. Not too much money,' she added, in case I thought she was going to hand over a hundred-euro note. Which I didn't. Anyway, I thought that was very nice of her, and it shows she appreciates my musical talents.

MONDAY ☀

So it turns out Cass isn't the only gay person at the summer camp. I mean, obviously she isn't – there are over a hundred people there so it stands to reason a few of them would be gay. But she says it is strangely comforting to know for sure that they are there. Or at least that one of them is. After lunch today, Ellie took Cass to look at some of the props in the art room (Cass is still yearning for the world of set design), and when Alice, Jane and I were on our way back from the canteen, we bumped into Jamie from the drama course. Even though he is two years older than us, unlike SOME people (Rachel) he has manners and is able to talk politely to people younger than him. We were just chatting about our various courses, and Alice said something about being glad Richard was doing the course too.

'It's not like we're joined at the hip or anything,' she said. 'But it's fun that we're all involved in the same big thing.'

'Yeah, I wish my boyfriend was here too,' said Jamie. 'But he's doing a computer-programming thing in Trinity for secondary-school students. Which is cool, obviously, but it would be handy if it was here too.'

'I didn't know you had a boyfriend!' said Jane.

Jamie grinned. 'Yeah, I do,' he said. 'You're not shocked, are you?'

'Hardly,' said Jane, looking offended at the very thought.

'Well, you'd be surprised,' said Jamie. 'Or, actually, you probably wouldn't.' He looked at me and Alice. 'You're doing the rock camp thing, right? A few of your fellow band people had some charming words for me the other day.'

'Ugh, I bet I know who that was,' I said. 'Was it a really cocky boy with sort of light brown hair with too much gel?'

'It was,' said Jamie. Charlie. Of course. 'I don't think he even knows I'm gay. He and his red-haired friend were calling my friend Cillian gay too, and he's got a girlfriend.'

He certainly does. That's the boy Ellie fancies. But it seems that Charlie (and his bandmate Robbie – I presume that's who the red-haired pal was) just uses 'gay' as a general sort of insult to any boy who isn't exactly like him, ie a boring toad. Anyway, when we found Cass again, we told her about Jamie. I didn't want it to look like we thought she would automatically bond with him just because they're both gay, but I did think she'd be interested, and she was. He is the first teenager she has encountered besides Liz who is actually out.

Speaking of Liz, she is home today, and Cass was going into town after the camp to meet her. Apparently, her mum wanted her to invite Liz over to their house so she could meet her properly (they met at our musical, but of course Liz wasn't Cass's girlfriend then), but Cass refused because she knows her mum would just be fussing over them the whole time and saying how cool it is to have a lesbian daughter. I don't blame her (Cass, not her mum). It was bad enough when John met my parents for the first time, and I didn't have to worry about them going on about how open-minded they were for five hours.

Anyway, Cass could hardly concentrate today because she is so excited at the thought of their big reunion. I really am happy for her, though I couldn't help wishing I'd ever got to have a big reunion with Paperboy. Sometimes I used to imagine that he had come home without telling me and I'd just open the door and find him there. And just imagining that moment would make me feel really happy, just for a second. I suppose he will come back to Dublin at some stage, at least for a visit – I mean, all his grandparents and aunts and uncles and stuff are still here, and he's not going to stay in Canada for the rest of his life. But it wouldn't be the same now.

Anyway, I really am happy for Cass. Honestly. And she managed to calm down for our great workshop this afternoon, which was just us and Kitty. We did some recording in the campus studio, which was more complicated than you'd think but still good fun. We recorded some of the instruments separately, which was quite weird, and then we each sang our vocals. And now we have a rough version of 'The Real Me!' It's mad hearing a recorded version. It actually makes us sound more professional than I thought it would. Imagine, in a few years, when we are famous rock stars (and possibly famous TV chefs too if the whole sweet-making thing works out), maybe this recording will be worth a fortune! I said this to Alice, and she said that it mightn't be worth a fortune, exactly, but our fans would treasure it. Which is good enough.

TUESDAY ☾

I got my exam results! And after all my panicking, I did quite well: two As, mostly Bs, and a C in maths. The others did well too – in fact, Cass did better in maths than I did. She was in a very good mood today, not only because she won't have to go to extra maths classes but also because she has had her joyous reunion with Liz. She was practically skipping along the corridors. I was worried she wouldn't be able to give any attention to the band, but I have to say that she was very hardworking once we were in the practice space this morning. She even came up with a great bassline for a new song, which led Alice to work out a gorgeous catchy melody. It's really good. I'm going to write some lyrics for it so we can perfect it in time for our show next week.

Actually, I have a new source of inspiration for my lyric-writing, because we had another excellent songwriting workshop with Ian Cliff today. He seems nice, but he is rather intimidating. (I think that is because he is so tall. Oh God, maybe Cass and Alice are right and I really do have a thing about tall people? Surely not. I mean, anyone would be intimidated by Ian Cliff, he's practically a giant.) He played a few different songs, and we had to analyse them to see how they worked. It was very interesting. There is a thing in songs called a middle eight which is a bit that doesn't have exactly the same tune or chords as the chorus or the verse. We realised that none of our songs have a middle eight, so after the workshop we went back to our practice room and basically added one to the song we've been working on – we took a verse from another song we'd started recently that went quite well with the chords. Our songwriting skills really are developing.

The only thing that spoiled the day was, unsurprisingly, Charlie and his disgusting Crack Parrots. They were talking about Jamie. They have discovered that he actually is gay – probably by eavesdropping on other people's conversations, it's not like they talk much to anyone else on the course apart from when they're bragging about how great they are. Anyway, I was sitting in front of them at the workshop, and at one stage, when Ian was talking to Small Paula about something (they both looked very intense and mysterious – they have quite a lot in common even though they are such different heights), I couldn't help eavesdropping myself because they were laughing about Jamie at top volume.

'He actually has a boyfriend,' said Charlie, putting on a stupid high-pitched voice as he said the last word. And they all laughed like this was in some way funny.

'I bet you it's that Cillian,' said Robbie. 'I saw him carrying around some paintbrushes yesterday. He's so gay.'

That is not only obnoxious and hateful, it makes no sense at all. Why would carrying around paintbrushes be gay? Does that mean all artists and decorators are gay? It's ridiculous. I was going to turn around and say something to them but then Ian Cliff left Small Paula and started talking to the entire workshop so I couldn't. He started talking about the power of political songwriting, which made me realise that this is something Hey Dollface could look into. So far all our songs have been about personal woes. But maybe we should turn our attention to the wider world. I mean, thanks to Miss Kelly we definitely know a lot about climate change. I will think more about this.

WEDNESDAY ❀

So ... I think I might have been wrong about Lucy. In fact, I know I was. I feel a bit stupid. Especially for wondering if she was jealous because she thought I was after Sam. But really, she was a bit silly too.

Here's what happened. The camp was great today. We had a really good workshop with Eli Gavroche about mixing up musical genres. And Niall from Puce was trying out another new look. He was wearing a sort of headband, and I think he almost pulled it off. Of course, I heard Charlie and Co dropping stupid comments, but Niall didn't seem to care, which is cool.

Anyway, afterwards I set off into town to get a present for Rachel like the good sister I am. So, after bidding farewell to my pals, I headed over to the bus stop. When I saw Lucy waiting there, my stomach dropped. It's not like I didn't like her, as I said. It's just I always feel – or at least, I felt – awkward around her, because I think – or thought – she didn't like me. And I knew I couldn't avoid talking to her at the bus stop because we do know each other now, even though we've never actually talked on our own before. Also, she was the only person at the bus stop. Anyway, as I approached the stop, I raised my hand in greeting but she looked straight past me, as usual. And just as I was starting to feel annoyed and insulted, she rummaged around in her bag, took out a pair of rather nice glasses and put them on. Then she looked straight at me in a surprised way and said, 'Oh, hi!'

'Hey,' I said. And then, because I couldn't think of anything else to say, I said, 'I didn't know you wore glasses.'

Lucy looked embarrassed.

'Oh, yeah,' she said. 'I do.'

'Do you just need them for reading or something?' I said.

Lucy looked a bit pink.

'Um, not exactly,' she said. 'I ... I'm actually pretty short-sighted.'

'Oh,' I said, confused. 'So why don't you wear your specs? At the camp, I mean.'

'Ah,' said Lucy. 'I've sort of stopped wearing them. I mean, I decided I wasn't going to wear them at the summer camp.'

'Really?' I said. 'Um, but why?'

Lucy looked even more embarrassed. 'I just ... I dunno.' She took a deep breath. 'I knew I was going to be meeting loads of new people, and I didn't want to be thought of as "someone who wears glasses". I wanted to start afresh.'

I can understand wanting to start afresh. After all, I did get that fringe. But this seemed like a rather drastic way of doing it. My fringe might look ridiculous (though I really think it might actually be getting longer at last), but at least I can still, you know, see.

'But no one thinks like that!' I said. 'Just look at Cass. She has glasses, and she looks cool. Doesn't she?'

'Yeah, she does,' said Lucy. 'And I know it's stupid. I just thought I'd look better without them. Although I can't really tell, because I can't see myself in the mirror unless I'm right next to it.'

'Well, you do look good without them,' I said. 'But you look just as good with them! They're really nice glasses.'

'Thanks,' said Lucy. 'Oh, I dunno. I just feel people see me as, you know, a specky person. And I wanted to see what it'd be like if they didn't.'

'Is there a big difference?' I said.

'Not really,' she said. 'Apart from not being able to see things if they're, like, a metre away from me. I'm starting to think it was a pretty stupid idea.'

A thought struck me.

'So does this mean that you can't see people properly, in the corridors and stuff?' I said.

'Yeah,' said Lucy. 'Oh God, have I been ignoring you?'

'Well, kind of,' I admitted.

'Oh no,' said Lucy. 'I'm so sorry. Sam said this would happen. But I was sure I wasn't quite that blind. I mean, I can recognise people when they're right next to me. It's just hard to focus on their faces.'

'You did sometimes look as if you were staring over my shoulder,' I admitted.

'Oh God,' said Lucy. She buried her face in her hands. 'I'm a total fool.'

'No, of course you're not,' I said. 'I do understand. But how have you managed to do all the drawing in the art course if you can't see?'

'I just lean right over the page,' said Lucy. 'Things almost look better that way, so I don't mind.' She sighed. 'It all sounds so silly when I say it out loud.'

So there you go. Lucy isn't rude. She was just trying to reinvent herself. And yes, she did it in a rather silly way, but I can understand where she was coming from. Just as I dreamed of starting the camp as a person with a glossy new fringe, she dreamed of starting it as a person without specs. Anyway, we had a really good chat on the bus. She is definitely not into Sam. She says they are like brother and sister because they have been friends since they were tiny. I did not bring this up, by the way. She did because she was talking about some of the boys on the course and said the only downside of her friendship with Sam is that people tend to think they are a couple. Which has been annoying when either of them actually likes someone else. Not that I think she really does like anyone else on the course. At least there are two of us.

Anyway, this all meant that what I thought would be a very awkward bus journey stuck talking to someone I didn't think liked me was actually pretty fun. I might even have made another new friend. I told her about having to buy Rachel a birthday present, and she suggested this really nice, cool nail varnish you can only get in one shop in the Jervis Centre so I decided to get Rachel that and a book. Which I think is a good balance of presents. AND she's getting my song as well. I truly am a much more noble sister than Rachel. I can't even remember what she got me last year.

LATER

Just remembered that Rachel actually got me a really nice top for my birthday last year. Hmmm. Perhaps she isn't so bad after all.

LATER

Also, it is my birthday in a few weeks so hopefully when I give her the nice present it will inspire her to get me something even better.

THURSDAY ◎

Lucy wore her glasses in the camp today. She said she felt a bit stupid going around without them now I knew she couldn't see properly. I think she thought other people were going to stare or make a fuss but, actually, people hardly noticed, apart from a few 'Oh, cool glasses' or, of course, 'I didn't know you wore glasses.' If we knew each other better, I would have been tempted to point out that really she should have done this two and a half weeks ago, but I knew it wouldn't make her feel any better so I didn't say anything.

In other news, we got the line-ups for our shows next week. Richard's band are one of the first to play, on Wednesday – the same day as the Crack Parrots (ugh). We're playing with both the Paulas (Tall and Small) on Friday, the very last day. Which is kind of cool, because I think if we were doing it on, say, Thursday, the last day would feel a bit anticlimactic. And this also gives us even more time to perfect our songs, including all the new ones we've written over the course of the camp.

Oh, and Rachel loved her birthday present (I thanked Lucy for the polish recommendation today). After I presented her with the physical part of it this morning, I wasn't sure I was going to sing her the song. After all, I had really only come up with it because I wasn't going to spend money on a present. We are not usually a family who declare our affection for each other seriously. But then I thought of how much time I'd spent on it and it seemed like a bit of a waste not to actually sing it.

'I have an extra present too,' I said. 'It's a special song, written just for you. Just don't take it too seriously,' I added, lest all my praise go to her head. And I sang it to her. I tried my best not to sound sarcastic, but it was quite difficult as I don't praise her very often. But it was her birthday and I had gone to the trouble of writing it. She had a strange look on her face, and I had a funny feeling she was going to start laughing, but, at the end, she seemed quite pleased and gave me a hug.

'I could even record it for you if you like,' I said. 'We've still got a fair bit of studio time at the camp.'

'Oh, that's all right,' said Rachel. 'Your beautiful live singing is enough.' She was joking, but I didn't mind. I suppose she is okay really.

And, speaking of my songs, I've written some lyrics for that song we were working on on Tuesday. It's called 'Living in a Bubble', and it's my first song with a political theme. I think it is quite powerful.

The planet is in trouble

But you're living in a bubble

And I'm not sure that you mind

You don't care for the environment

You're worse than any government

Can you really be that blind?

CHORUS

Polar bears and giant waves

We've got a big old world to save

Polar bears and giant waves

If we can't save the world, we'll have to live in caves

The honey bees are dying

When they should be out there flying

But I'm not sure that you care

The weather's going mad

But you think it's just a fad

Not a terrible nightmare

CHORUS

Polar bears and giant waves

We've got a big old world to save
Polar bears and giant waves
If we can't save the world, we'll have to live in caves

We've got to take it seriously
Although we haven't previously
We can't let those bears and bees die
So you've got to listen to our cry

Reduce, reuse, recycle
And ride an old bicycle
That's what you've got to do
Stop wasting everything
And living like a king
And the world just might pull through

CHORUS
Polar bears and giant waves
We've got a big old world to save
Polar bears and giant waves
If we can't save the world, we'll have to live in caves

Note that there is a middle eight (the bit about 'We've got to take it seriously'). Our songwriting is definitely evolving. And I am quite proud of the honey-bee bit. It was inspired by a thing I read in my parents' paper at the weekend about how bees are dying because of some mysterious bee plague, and while this might not seem like a huge environmental disaster (although of course it is very sad for the poor bees), it actually is terrible for all of us because bees pollinate loads of flowers and plants and so basically we are dependent on them for everything from apples to, of course, honey. Anyway, I am glad that I've been able to highlight their tragic plight in song. I will try it out on the others tomorrow.

FRIDAY ☺

Brilliant day. First of all, we got loads of work done in the practice space today. The others like my song lyrics. In fact, Alice said she thought Miss Kelly would be proud of my green message, and I think she is right. Maybe if we play it to her when we go back to school in September, it would prove that our creative projects aren't a total waste of time?

And second of all, we had our second Crack Parrots-free day in a row, because we were all in our own studios in the morning and in the afternoon they were in another workshop (for once). So we were able to enjoy our sound-engineering workshop with Dave Crewe without Charlie and his gang making not-so-smart remarks all the time. It was great.

Also, a bunch of us went into town after the camp today, which was really good fun – us Hey Dollfacers and the Wicked Ways and Jane and her drama friend Gemma, and Ellie and Sam and Lucy. We ended up taking over half a coffee shop, and we stayed until it closed and they kicked us out. The staff looked pleased to get rid of us. I think it was because we'd been there for, like, two hours and only ordered one drink each. But it's not our fault they charge so much for a boring beverage. Anyway, we all had a very good chat about our creative ambitions. Jane and Gemma have decided to write a play together.

'I always thought I wanted to be on stage,' said Jane. 'But actually I think I might want to work behind the scenes.'

'I can make your sets,' said Cass. 'When I'm not being a famous rock star, of course.'

'Or a sweet-maker,' I said, and we told the others about our fudge-making plans. They were very impressed and asked if we'd bring in samples, but we said they'd have to wait until the giveaway at our gig next week. We need to build up the hype. About both the band and the sweets.

Oh, and I had a really good chat with Sam about books and comics. I gave him back *Good Omens* (which I loved, it was so funny and exciting and scary), and he lent me one of the *Sandman* graphic novels (which is basically a comic). I've finished it already, because you can read a graphic really quickly what with most of it being pictures. I have been reading it since I got home and it is very good but a bit freaky. I hope it doesn't give me weird dreams. Especially as I have to get up early tomorrow because I am going into town with Cass and Liz. I haven't seen Liz since she and Cass started going out, so I hope it won't be awkward and I won't be some weird gooseberry. I can't imagine it will be, but you never know.

SATURDAY ☺

Today's outing with Cass and Liz wasn't awkward at all. In fact, it was really good fun. At first, getting used to the idea

that Liz is Cass's girlfriend, not just her friend, felt a bit odd –
not really because she's a girl, though actually seeing Cass with
a girlfriend was a bit strange at first. But it was mostly because
I'm not used to Cass going out with anyone, male or female,
so seeing her holding hands with someone is a bit surprising.
And even though I've known about her being with someone
for the past few weeks, it's just been in theory, not in practice.
If you know what I mean.

But the feeling of oddness didn't last very long. We met outside the gates of Trinity, and when Liz arrived she grinned at me
and said, 'Hey Bex! So Cass told you all about our forbidden
love.'

And I laughed and said she had, and I joked about how
shocked I was. And then everything was normal. I have found
that once you find yourself laughing together at something
it sort of stops things being awkward. We all went for hot
chocolate, and Liz told me about the Gaeltacht. She said she'd
been a bit worried about going away with Katie because Katie
was so weird when she first came out.

'But it was okay in the end,' she said. 'We were in the
same house, and the other girls all knew each other so we
had to stick together. She's totally cool about everything

now. We were dancing together hand in hand at all the ceilís by the end of it.'

It sounds like she had a really good time. It made me wish that the North Dublin Arts Camp wasn't just a twenty-minute walk from my house. It'd be lots of fun if we could all go away and stay somewhere. Although Liz said that she had no internet access, and the food was pretty terrible, and she did get homesick every so often. So maybe it wasn't all so great.

Anyway, it was a really fun afternoon. And I didn't feel gooseberryish at all. We went to one of the music shops on Exchequer Street and tried loads of instruments. I had a lot of fun bashing away on a giant drum kit, and Cass tried some really cool keyboards that can make loads of brilliant sounds. Liz tried some gorgeous guitars. She is very good at playing the guitar, even better than Alice.

'But I've been playing the electric guitar for years, because my big sister has one,' she said. 'So I've had lots of practice. Oh, look at this sparkly one! Why is it so expensive? Why? Cass, darling Cass, please let you and Bex and Alice make lots of money from your home-made sweet empire, and then you can lavish me with glittery guitars.'

'If we make any money from our empire, I will lavish myself

with keyboards first,' said Cass. 'Sorry!'

'But we could give you one if we have any profits left over after lavishing ourselves,' I said. 'Oh, and Alice too, because if we have fancy new instruments she'll need one as well.'

'This is true,' said Cass. 'Otherwise the band will sound terrible.'

'Fair enough,' said Liz. 'I'll just have to think of a way of earning my own fortune.'

We talked about ways in which Liz could make money as Cass and I walked her to her bus stop on Nassau Street (in the end, she thought she could try knitting things and selling them because she made 'quite a good scarf once', although she was only ten at the time, so she might be a bit rusty). In the meantime, she is going to call over to my house during the week to help us make some fudge to give away at our final show on Friday. We had just reached the side entrance to Trinity when she saw a number 15 approaching.

'Oops, that's me, I'd better run,' she said. 'Bye Cass!' she said. And she gave Cass a quick hug and kiss on the lips. Then she cried, 'Bye, Bex!' And with a cheery wave, she ran for the bus.

'I'm glad she's back,' said Cass, happily.

'So am I,' I said. 'Just because it's stopped you moping. You've been moping all over the place recently.'

'Oh shut up, moping expert,' said Cass, but we knew she didn't mean it. 'Ugh, look who it is lurking across the road – over there, at the end of Dawson Street!'

It was evil Charlie. I think he saw us, but we pretended we didn't see him and stayed on the other side of the road while he walked on in the other direction. He's so obnoxious, and we have enough of him at the camp. I don't want to have to put up with his 'banter' at the weekends too. But besides seeing Charlie, it was a really fun afternoon. I feel strangely relieved. I was a bit scared that Cass and Liz being together would mean I'd never see Cass over the rest of the holidays, but I don't think that now. Like, obviously they'll want to do stuff on their own sometimes, but I know we'll be able to hang out together too.

It did make me wish I had someone too, though. I mean, I've been at a camp full of boys for three weeks now, and I still don't fancy any of them. I really am starting to worry that I'll never meet anyone I like ever again. I mean, everyone seems to be all settled now. Look at Rachel and Saint Tom, the perfect boyfriend; they've been together for over a year, and I can't imagine them ever splitting up. Maybe Paperboy and John Kowalski were my only shot at romance and now the rest of my life will be loveless. It is a depressing thought. I wish I could just fall in love with someone. Who liked me too, obviously.

On a happier note, my godmother Daisy is taking me out to lunch tomorrow as an advance birthday present (it's not my birthday for almost a month, but she's going on holiday soon so she won't be around then). So that should be fun, even though that baby of hers will probably get sick on me, as it usually does whenever we meet. I thought it might improve with age but it certainly hasn't so far.

SUNDAY ☼

I had a very nice lunch with Daisy today, and it has made me feel a lot better about life in general. Who would have thought one lunch could do that? But it has. Even though the baby got sick on me yet again. Why does it keep doing this to me? What did I ever do to it? I suggested to Daisy that it might have some sort of terrible stomach bug, but she said it just throws up its milk every so often (mostly on me, apparently), and it should stop doing that soon because it's going to start eating solid human food. I'll believe that when I see it.

Anyway, I met Daisy (and the bad baby) in town, and she took me to a lovely restaurant. I hardly ever get to go out for proper food because my parents are such misers (or, as they put it, 'we're not made of money') so just going to the restaurant on its own would have made me feel better. Especially as the baby slept most of the way through lunch.

Once we were seated at our table and had ordered our food, Daisy asked me about the summer camp, and I told her all about Kitty and all the bands and the drama and art people and how fun it was. Talking to Daisy is not like talking to Mum. Which is strange because she's only a few years younger than her, ie very old.

'So it sounds like you're having an excellent summer,' said Daisy. 'You are, right?'

'Well, yeah,' I said. 'But ...'

And then somehow I found myself telling her all the stuff I'd been secretly thinking for weeks. About how the others were going out with people and how I didn't fancy anyone and I was worried I'd never meet anyone I liked ever again. I realised I'd never actually talked about this to anyone, because the only people I could have been so sorry for myself in front of are Cass and Alice, and in this case I didn't feel I could say anything to them because they might feel sorry for me and that was the worst thing I could imagine. But I didn't really mind Daisy feeling sorry for me. It was such a relief to finally say all this to another person.

'And really, there are no fanciable boys at all on the whole course,' I finished sadly.

Daisy looked very concerned.

'So are your friends making you feel left out?' she said.

'Well, no, not really,' I said. 'Actually not at all. I don't feel bad when I'm with them. But when I go home, I sort of feel left out, like they're a part of something and I'm not. Do you know what I mean?'

'Sort of,' said Daisy. 'But everything's fine when you're all together, right? And you like their boyfriends – boyfriend and girlfriend, I mean?'

'Well, yeah,' I said. 'I mean, they haven't abandoned me or anything. They'd never do that. And I do really like Richard and Liz.'

'So, let me get this straight,' said Daisy. 'Even though your best friends are going out with people, they're not making you feel left out. You still see them all the time. And you like the people they're going out with. You don't feel weird hanging out with them. They don't make you feel uncomfortable or awkward, or anything.'

'I suppose so,' I said. 'Well, yeah.'

'And, in general, you're having lots of fun and you're doing lots of cool and exciting things,' said Daisy.

'Um, yes,' I said. 'I suppose.'

'So what's the actual problem?' said Daisy.

When she put it like that, I wasn't actually sure.

'I dunno,' I said. 'I think it's just that sometimes I worry that I'll never find love again. Like, Paperboy and John Kowalski were it and I'll never go out with anyone else.'

And Daisy just burst out laughing, which I found quite annoying at the time, not least because it woke up the baby, and it started roaring (its favourite activity after getting sick on me). But what she said once the baby had been calmed down made me less annoyed.

'Bex,' she said. 'You're not even fifteen.'

'I'm almost fifteen,' I said. 'I'll be fifteen in a few weeks.'

'It doesn't matter,' said Daisy. 'You're very young. When I

was your age I hadn't gone out with anyone. In fact, I didn't even kiss anyone until I was seventeen. And I ended up not going out with anyone until I was in college.'

'But did that ... did it bother you?' I said.

'Yes!' said Daisy. 'It did. I used to worry about it all the time. I was worried that I'd never meet anyone. I was worried there was something horribly wrong with me. But there wasn't! Everything was fine in the end. I just wish I hadn't wasted so much time worrying about it. There was no hurry.'

'It kind of feels like there is,' I said. 'Sometimes.'

'Well, there isn't,' said Daisy. 'Oh my God, Bex, you're really lucky. You have really good friends, and you've got your band and your writing and lots of cool stuff that you're interested in. It looks like your only problem is that you're worrying about never going out with anyone ever again. And that isn't going to happen.'

'I suppose so,' I said. 'Though it's not my only problem. I mean, my parents are pretty annoying. I know they're your friends and everything, but they are.'

'Believe me, Bex,' said Daisy. 'Your parents are okay. And even if they do annoy you, your life is fine.'

And as she said it, I believed her. Well, apart from the bit about my parents being okay. If my mum had been talking to me like this, I wouldn't have taken her seriously, but somehow it's different with Daisy. And she's right, I suppose I am quite lucky. After all, my friends are going out with people I like who don't make me feel like a total gooseberry when we're all hanging out together. I have a horrible feeling that John Kowalski wasn't like that at all. In fact, I remember the way he used to act when Cass walked down the road with us after school, and I know he wasn't.

Anyway, we didn't just talk about my romantic problems (or lack of them). We also talked about my parents. Daisy said she can't wait to see the musical next week.

'Really?' I said.

'I wouldn't miss it for the world!' she said. 'I'm going to go on Sunday, the second night. I told you before, your mum was poetry in motion flying around that stage in the *Pirates of Penzance*. And *so* was your dad when he did his dance solo! He caused a sensation.'

I am sure he did, though I don't think it was in a good way.

'Are you sure?' I said.

'Of course I am,' said Daisy. 'He was brilliant. Like I said, poetry in motion. I just wish they both had bigger parts in this production of *Oliver!*. It's a shame to waste all that talent at the chorus.'

I almost wish she hadn't said this. After all, if she is so clearly mistaken about my parents' theatrical abilities, can I really trust her romantic advice? But I think my parents might be her one weakness. I mean, she's an actual theatre critic, and those newspapers wouldn't keep employing her if she was always praising terrible things. She must just have a blind spot when it comes to my parents. They've all been great mates for a million years, after all. I mean, if Cass and Alice were in a musical being terrible I might be blinded by friendship too (although I am not being biased when I say they can both definitely dance better than my dad).

Anyway, I feel a lot better about, well, everything now. In fact, right now the only thing that's bothering me is the thought of Mrs Harrington. There really is no way I can change Mum's mind at this stage. I'm just going to have to pray Mrs Harrington suddenly decides she hates my mum's books and never reads the new one. Although I don't think this is very likely.

MONDAY ☼

Guess who I met in the shops on my way home from summer camp today? Mrs Harrington! And I think everything might be okay now. I can't believe she just appeared after I was thinking about her last night. It is like I have magical powers. Although if I did, then Paperboy would have come back from Canada a long time ago because I certainly thought more about him than I did about Mrs Harrington.

Anyway, it all happened like this. I was on my own because Alice had to get a lift early today and Cass was going into town to meet Liz, and I thought I'd pop into the Spar to get a Dairy Milk. And who should be coming out of the shop as I was going in but Mrs Harrington. She looked delighted to see me, but I'm pretty sure I did not look delighted to see her. Because I wasn't.

'Rebecca!' she cried. She didn't seem to feel at all embarrassed at meeting one of her pupils outside of school. 'And how are you? Are you having a nice holiday?'

'Um, I'm fine,' I said. 'I'm doing the summer arts camp down in the college.'

'Good, good,' she said. And then, before I could get away,

she asked the one question I was hoping she wouldn't ask.

'And how's your mammy's book coming along?' she said. 'I can't wait to read all about Patricia Alexandra! What sort of thing does she get up to?'

And I was going to pretend I didn't know, but then ... Well, maybe it was because of all the revelations of the last month, but I suddenly thought, 'I have to tell the truth'. Admittedly, I first thought this months ago and really should have followed through on it back then, but, anyway, better late than never. If Cass could tell me she's gay even when she was scared I'd never talk to her again, I could tell Mrs Harrington what the fictional Patricia Alexandra is like. Now I come to think of it, the real truth would be admitting that Mum never promised to put her in a book at all. But that would be going a bit too far. Surely this bit of truth was enough for now?

So anyway, I took a deep breath and said, 'Well, actually, Mrs Harrington, she's done something a bit ... funny with Patricia Alexandra Harrington.'

'Oh, really?' said Mrs Harrington, looking very pleased.

'Yes,' I said. 'Um, she decided it would be more ... interesting if she made her, um, a sort of a, well, a villain. I mean, it would be very different from the real thing. I mean you. But anyway ... basically Patricia Alexandra is a teacher, but she's the heroine's enemy, and she's really horrible. She tries to ruin the heroine's life and everything.'

I looked up nervously at Mrs Harrington. I expected her to be appalled that her idol – my mother – had given her name to an evil, life-ruining teacher. But to my amazement, she didn't look appalled. She looked absolutely delighted.

'Oh, that's wonderful!' she said. 'I can't wait to tell Gerard!'

'What?' I said. 'You're not ... annoyed?'

'Not at all!' said Mrs Harrington. 'Some of my favourite Rosie Carberry characters are the baddies! They're always so memorable. Don't you just love Elizabeth Battersby in *The Girl from Braddon Hall*? Who stole that poor girl's business? And Angela Hayden from *Family Sorrows, Family Joys*? The way she convinced poor Imelda that Tony didn't really love her ...'

'I ... suppose so,' I said, even though I couldn't remember anything about any of these people because Mum's books are all the same to me.

'Now, I hope my namesake has her comeuppance,' said Mrs Harrington playfully. 'I don't want her to get away with her crimes!'

201

'Well, I don't want to spoil it for you,' I said. 'But I'm sure she won't. Get away with it, I mean.'

Though it seems that I have got away with concocting my terrible web of lies. Which even I have to admit isn't very fair and doesn't fit in with Ellie's mum's theory that every bad deed gets punished in the end. But I'm certainly not complaining. Anyway, I have learned a lesson. Sort of. I'm never going to tell crazy lies to a teacher ever again.

I eventually got away from Mrs Harrington, who would happily have spent the entire day going on about various villains from my mother's books, and went home in a daze. I couldn't believe I'd been worrying about this for ages for no real reason! I was so amazed by it all that when I got in and Mum gave out to me for dropping my jacket on the couch, I didn't even argue with her. In fact, I felt quite kindly towards her, because it turns out that she has done just the right thing to make Mrs Harrington happy, without even knowing it.

'Hey Mum,' I said, as I hung up my jacket on the coat rack. 'You know I came up with that name, Patricia Alexandra Harrington?'

'Of course,' said Mum. 'And I'm very grateful. I don't think that character would have worked with another name.

You basically created her!'

'Well, actually it turns out one of my teachers has the same name,' I said. 'I bumped into her today, and it sort of ... came up. I must have seen her full name written down somewhere, and that's what put it into my subconscious mind.'

Mum looked horrified.

'Oh no!' she said. 'Oh my God, I'll have to change it. She'll think it's after her.' She looked really worried. 'Sorry, love. I know you didn't pick her name on purpose so it's not your fault ...'

'No, don't worry!' I said. 'I told her the character was horrible and she was really pleased! She loves your books, and she especially loves the baddies! So it's a good thing! She'd be really sad if you changed the name.'

'Really?' said Mum. 'Are you totally sure?'

'Of course,' I said. 'I'd hardly lie about something like this, would I? I mean, I have to go back to school and be taught by her in September.'

'Hmmm,' said Mum. 'Maybe I should try and contact her through your school just to be sure ...'

'Oh, no, don't make a fuss,' I said. 'But if you could thank her in the acknowledgements, I bet she'd be really happy. Her and her husband, Gerard. He loves your books too.'

'Okay,' said Mum. 'That's a relief.'

She can't be as relieved as I am. I know I should have told her the whole story about me promising Mrs Harrington that she'd put her in a book and all that. But surely that would be more trouble than it is worth?

TUESDAY ☾

The world of showbiz has had a terrible effect on my dad. He's always been a basically decent human being, but that musical has made him surprisingly callous. Tonight Rachel and I were sitting on the couch happily watching *Laurel Canyon* when my parents arrived home from their *Oliver!* rehearsal full of excitement.

'Great news!' said Dad. 'Philip Judge is in hospital!'

'Ed!' said my mum, horrified.

'What?' said Rachel.

'Who is Philip Judge?' I said. 'And why is this good news?'

Dad instantly looked ashamed of himself.

'Um, I didn't mean that the way it sounded,' he said. 'It's

not good for him, obviously. And he's fine!' he added anxiously. 'I mean, he hasn't died. I'm not revelling in someone's death. Or, you know, serious illness. He's grand. They thought he was having a heart attack, but it was just angina, so he just has to take it easy for a few weeks.'

'But who is he?' said Rachel.

'He was playing the Beadle in *Oliver!*,' said Dad. 'And now he can't do the show. And I'm his understudy. Which means ...'

'It means your dad gets to take over the part on Saturday,' said Mum. 'Though he needn't announce it quite so gleefully!'

'Sorry,' said Dad, looking abashed. 'You know I wouldn't be happy if he was really sick.'

I'd like to think he wouldn't be, but to be honest I'm not completely sure right now. He's certainly very excited about stepping into poor Mr Judge's shoes. Both my parents are taking this musical worryingly seriously. They spent the rest of the night in the front room going through Dad's new part, even though he knows all the words already.

Though maybe there is something about the theatre that sends people a bit mad. Jane and the others are very excited about their play, which we will finally get to see on Thursday. I thought Vanessa and Karen would have driven her insane by now, but she keeps saying that when it comes to the play they're just really focused on their work.

At lunchtime today, she was sitting at a table with Gemma and Bernard the Fairy-tale Prince, and when Alice and I went to join them we found them all talking very intensely about the play.

'But if the dragon comes on then, it'll change the dynamic between the girls in the hospital,' Jane was saying.

'We've only got two more days,' said Gemma. 'If it's not working now, we'll have to think of something else for that scene. Maybe we could move the knife juggling around a bit? Or the fireworks?'

I am quite impressed that they have gone for such a challenging project, as I said to Alice later.

'Hmmm,' said Alice. 'I'm not sure the fireworks are a good idea. I mean, how good is Vanessa at juggling, really?'

'Well, she is full of surprises,' I said. 'Remember how shocked we were when we discovered she could actually act.'

'True,' said Alice. 'Vanessa is more complex than you'd think. She's quite mysterious, really.'

Really, just about everyone at this camp is better at being mysterious than I am. Though I wish Charlie was a bit more mysterious. Or at least kept his stupid mouth shut. At the end of the day, the Crack Parrots were lounging around on the sofas in the arts building, and just as we were walking past I heard Charlie say, 'Did you see your man Jamie today? What the hell was he wearing?'

'The state of him!' said Robbie, sniggering. All the Crack Parrots snigger. It's the only way to describe the horrible way they laugh at everyone who isn't a total moron like them.

'Ah, come on, Jamie's okay,' said Evan. There was silence, until he added, 'Though he dresses like a total ...' And then he said a horrible word that I won't even write down here. And the rest of them all laughed.

'God,' said Cass after we'd left the building. 'Never having to see those goons again is the only good thing about the camp being over on Friday.'

She is right. But I can't believe there are only a few days left. I will miss it a LOT. The first of the band showcases is on tomorrow after the workshops, and Richard's band are going to be the first one on. He told us today he is planning to 'give it loads' on stage. I can only imagine what that will involve. He was quite intense at the Battle of the Bands and that was before he'd spent weeks with King of Intensity Ian Cliff. But I'm looking forward to it.

WEDNESDAY ❦

Something really horrible happened today. But also something pretty good. And overall, I think, goodness won. But the horrible bit was pretty bad. And, of course, it was all because of Charlie. I didn't think that I could hate him any more than I already did, but it turns out I can.

But I'd better go back to the beginning. The afternoon workshops had just finished, and a bunch of us from all the different classes – some of the bands and the artists and the drama people – were sitting on the big comfy couches in the foyer outside the theatre waiting for the stage to be set up for today's show. Richard was wearing his brother's suit again, which he had managed to find in the back of the spare room wardrobe where his brother had hidden it. (He is playing a dangerous game borrowing it. If his brother finds out about it he will be in a lot of trouble. Apparently his brother has threatened to steal and hide Richard's laptop if he ever takes the suit again. As I have found myself, older siblings are not very understanding about brothers or sisters borrowing stuff.) Anyway, Richard was all excited because at last he'll get to perform in front of his god, Ian Cliff.

'But you've played in front of him lots of times!' I said. 'Like, every day for the past three weeks!'

'You know that's not the same, Bex,' said Richard. 'There's a big difference between playing in a poky little rehearsal room full of chairs and amps and actually, like, rocking out on stage in front of an audience.'

Which is true, I suppose.

'It'll be good showing Kitty what we can do on Friday,' said Alice.

'As long as I don't fall off something,' I said gloomily.

'I don't think there'll be anything to fall off,' said Cass. 'The drums aren't on a platform this time. And you're hardly going to fall off the drum stool. Are you?'

'No!' I said. 'Of course not!'

'And even if you do fall off your stool,' said Ellie, 'you can just get back up and keep playing like you did last time! As long as you don't have, like, a concussion or something. Then you'd have to get to hospital straight away.'

'Oh thanks very much, that's very comforting,' I said.

That was when the Crack Parrots walked up.

'You on today too, Murray?' said Charlie.

'Yeah,' said Richard.

'Well, I hope your boyfriend Ian Cliff is impressed!' chortled Charlie. Richard just rolled his eyes and looked bored. Evan looked embarrassed, as well he might.

'That's really hilarious, Charlie,' said Cass drily.

'Oh, right, I might have known you'd stick up for that gaylord,' said Charlie.

Cass went a bit red, but she said, 'Seriously, Charlie, no one wants to listen to you. Go away.'

'Oh, what'll you do if I don't?' said Charlie. 'Get your girlfriend to beat me up?' Cass, Alice, Richard and I all stared at him, and he smirked horribly, like he'd just won some sort of battle. He looked ... triumphant.

'Yeah, I saw the pair of you in town on Saturday,' he said. 'You and your little lezzer friend holding hands and snogging in public! I might have known you were a dyke.'

When he said that horrible word I felt like I'd been slapped in the face, so I can only imagine how Cass felt. She went very white and started blinking in a way that means she was trying not to cry. I was so stunned and so angry I couldn't say anything for a second, but just as I was taking a breath to yell at Charlie, a very surprising voice roared, 'How DARE you say that to her!'

It was, of all people in the world, Karen Rodgers. I hadn't even noticed she was there, but she was pushing her way through the people sitting on the edge of the sofas, and she looked really, really angry. Cass and I looked at each other in amazement. For a moment, I think we were both more surprised than anything else.

'There's nothing wrong with being gay!' yelled Karen. 'And you should never call anyone that word!'

'Karen's right,' I said, and even now I can't believe those words actually came out of my mouth. 'You take that back right now and apologise to Cass.'

'Yeah,' said Cass. I could tell from her face that she was still really, really upset, but her voice didn't even wobble. 'Apologise now. You don't get to call me and my girlfriend that word.'

'Yeah, you don't,' said Alice.

Charlie literally sneered at us. I didn't think anyone did that outside of films.

'Oh right,' he laughed. 'Are you all lezzers, then? Should've guessed.'

God, he is so, so horrible.

'I'd rather be gay than a horrible bigot like you,' I said.

'Yeah,' said Richard, glaring at Charlie. 'So would I.'

'And so would I,' said Alice.

'And me,' said Sam.

'And me,' said Bernard the Fairy-tale Prince, who really is okay, I suppose.

'And me,' said Ellie and Lucy together.

'Me too,' said some girl from the art class who I don't know at all.

'And me,' said Tall Paula.

'Me too,' said Small Paula. Which is particularly impressive, as she hardly ever says anything.

And lots of other people joined in too. Not everyone, but enough to make it clear that most people were on Cass's side.

And THEN, as if Karen's outburst wasn't surprising enough, Evan said, 'And me. Seriously, dude, you're acting like a total arsehole. I don't want to be in a band with you anymore.'

Charlie looked genuinely taken aback. Then his usual cocky expression returned.

'Fine,' he said. 'Like I'd want to be in a band with another queer anyway.'

'Oh my God, Charlie, just SHUT UP,' said Evan. He was practically yelling. 'Why are you so obsessed with other people being gay? And why are you such a creepy dick to all the girls?

What's your problem? Just grow up!' And he grabbed his bass and stomped out of the room. The other members of Crack Parrots looked at each other.

'What's his problem, more like,' said Charlie, with a sort of snigger. 'It was just a bit of banter.'

Then, to my huge surprise, Finn got up.

'Sorry, Charlie,' said Finn. 'But Evan's right.' And he grabbed his drumsticks and walked after Evan. Robbie and Ryan, the other Crack Parrots' band member, stayed where they were, but they both looked pretty uncomfortable.

'Come on,' said Alice, looking coldly at Charlie and his two allies. 'They've opened the doors to the theatre now. Let's leave Charlie with all his many friends.' Which is quite bitchy for Alice, but totally justified in this case. And she grabbed me and Cass and marched into the theatre, Richard by our side. Pretty much everyone followed.

'You okay?' I said to Cass, who still looked a bit shaky and like she might start crying.

'Yeah, I think so,' said Cass in quite a wobbly voice. 'No, I am. Thanks for, well, you know. Standing up for me.'

'Oh, come on, Cass,' said Alice. 'As if we wouldn't!'

'But what about Karen?' I said. 'That was pretty surprising.

And, I have to admit, impressive.'

'Do I have to like Karen now?' said Cass, sounding worried. 'I think I might.'

'I think we all might,' I said. 'For a while, anyway. Or at least, like, accept that she's not totally evil really.'

'Oh well,' said Cass. 'I suppose I can live with that. Though I dunno if I can live with everyone staring at me. Is everyone staring at me?'

'Not really,' said Alice. 'I mean, I don't think anyone thinks it's a big deal. You're not the only gay person on the camp, after all.' Which was true. And there were a few funny looks, but they looked more curious than anything else. No one was really laughing or sniggering or whispering.

'And after what just happened, it really does look like everyone's on your side,' I said. 'Even Karen.'

'Oh, look, there she is,' said Cass. 'I suppose I'd better thank her now and get it over with. I'll feel bad if I don't. Hey, Karen!'

Karen came over, looking a bit embarrassed.

'Thanks,' said Cass. 'For, you know. What you said out there.'

Karen sort of shrugged. 'It's okay,' she said. 'Um, my aunt's gay, so I've always been kind of, I dunno, sensitive about that sort of thing.'

'Well, it was really nice of you,' said Cass.

'Thanks,' said Karen. 'I'll, um, see you later.' And she went off.

'Oof, that was awkward,' said Cass, with a big sigh.

'I'm sure things will get back to normal soon and she'll be doing our heads in again,' I said comfortingly. And I meant it. But I won't forget what Karen did today. She didn't have to stand up for Cass – she's not even her friend – but she did. I suppose she can't be all bad, even if she did spend all year tormenting me about my mum's book and then showing off about her great acting skills. The next time she does any of those things I'll just have to remind myself what she did today and tell myself she is a decent human being really. I have a feeling this will be very difficult, though. I mean, she really is quite annoying a lot of the time.

'Well, we can show our appreciation when they put on their play tomorrow,' said Alice.

'Oh yeah,' said Cass. 'I can't wait to see that. Wow. I'm looking forward to something involving Vanessa and Karen. This summer really has been full of surprises.'

Then – speak of the Devil – Vanessa came up to us.

'Is it true?' she demanded, without bothering to say hello, or anything vaguely polite. 'Are you, like, an actual lesbian?'

'Um, yes,' said Cass, looking taken aback. 'I suppose.'

'Oh right,' said Vanessa. 'That's cool.' And she walked off.

We all just stared at each other.

'Well, I don't think today could get any weirder,' said Cass.

'Come on, let's sit down before anything else peculiar can happen,' said Alice. Ellie, Sam and Lucy had saved us some seats, so we sat down just as the lights in the auditorium went down and Veronica walked on to the spotlit stage.

'Hey everybody,' she said. 'We've had a bit of a change to today's show – Crack Parrots won't be performing after all.' There were some cheers and a few boos and various yelling noises. Cass squirmed a bit in her seat between me and Alice. 'So we'd like you to give a big round of applause to our first act – Richard Murray and the Wicked Ways!'

Of course we all applauded and cheered like mad as Richard and the boys strode out. I had to admit that Richard did make the right decision to steal that suit. It looks really good on him. Not that I fancy him, I might add. Much as I like and, indeed, respect Richard, he just doesn't do anything for me. Which is a good thing, obviously, for many reasons.

Anyway, Richard grabbed the mike and said, in a voice that was about ten times lower than his usual voice, 'Hello, ladies and gentlemen. My name is Richard Murray, and these are the Wicked Ways. And our first song is called "The Fool".'

The drums and the bass kicked in, sounding impressively gloomy, then the guitar started playing a dramatic riff, and then Richard began to sing.

'I am ...' he sang, in a deep and rumbling voice, 'little more ... than a fooool.'

He has always been a bit ... melodramatic on stage, and somehow it always worked. But now he was taking it a bit further. Actually, make that a lot further. He was now hunched over so his chin nearly touched his knees.

'A fool ... for loooove ... a fool ... in life ...' he declaimed, still in the booming voice. Then he sprang upright again. 'Am I a fool to you?' he cried, flinging his arms wide. As the song went on, he stalked around the stage in a very dramatic fashion. At one stage, he shook his fist at the heavens. And then he lay down on the ground in order to roar the final chorus.

'I think he might have taken his love of Ian Cliff a bit too far,' I whispered to Cass.

'I think you're right,' said Cass. 'What's he doing now?

Is he … writhing?'

'Life!' roared Richard, still thrashing around on his back, 'has made a foooool of meeeeeeee!'

'I'm afraid he is,' I whispered back. 'Oh dear. We'd better shut up in case Alice hears us.'

Alice didn't seem to mind Richard's antics. In fact, she was staring at the stage in what looked like admiration. Love really must be blind. Eventually the song ended, with Richard still kicking about on the floor as he played the final bass notes, and there was a slightly stunned silence as he got to his feet. Then suddenly we heard loud clapping from up the front and a loud and even boomier voice than Richard had managed to achieve cried 'Bravo! Bravo!' It was, of course, Ian Cliff. It was like we'd been in a stunned trance until he started clapping, but then everyone else started joining in.

'Thank you, thank you,' said Richard. 'This next song is called "Odysseus", and I'd like to dedicate it to my friend Cass.'

'Oh God,' said Cass, but she tried to look pleased, because she knew Richard was being nice.

'Odysseus,' boomed Richard. 'You're a hero of the seven seas!'

Well, you can imagine the rest. The thing is, as the band went on, I started to get into it. I actually think Richard can pull this stuff off. Very few people could, without looking totally ridiculous. And of course he did look totally ridiculous. But he was somehow brilliant at the same time. The first time we saw the Wicked Ways, back at the Battle of the Bands, I said I thought he had star quality, and I was right. Cass felt the same way.

'Actually,' she said, halfway through 'Odysseus', 'am I going mad, or is this kind of cool?'

'You're not going mad,' I whispered back. When the band finished, we clapped and cheered with all our might. And by the end of their set, everyone was cheering and whooping. Ian Cliff even stood up.

'The Wicked Ways, everybody!' he shouted, and everyone cheered. Shane O'Driscoll cheered very loudly, which isn't surprising. His own music is very different to the Wicked Ways, but he obviously approved of Richard's dramatic gesturing. Even though Richard didn't do any actual prowling.

But when they had left the stage, something surprising happened. The stage lights were down, as they always are between acts, but after a while we could see something happening on stage. Shane O'Driscoll and some of the other mentors were pushing out two big packing cases onto the stage.

'Who's on now?' I asked.

'I think it's Puce,' said Alice. And it was. We could see the drummer, whose name I can never remember, getting into position, and then Niall walked onto the stage clutching his guitar. As the lights went on, he marched to the central mike at the front of the stage.

'Whoah,' said Cass. 'What is he wearing?'

'I think it's a jumpsuit,' said Alice. 'Or maybe a boiler suit. It kind of suits him!'

I'm not sure it did, but it certainly was eye-catching.

Then Niall grabbed the mike.

'We're Puce,' he cried. 'And we're here to rock your world!'

'Just him and the drummer?' whispered Cass in confusion. 'Where are the other two?'

But then Niall played his first chord, and two more spotlights hit the stage, shining straight onto the big packing cases. And, right on cue, the bass player and the other guitarist leaped up from behind the packing cases, where they must have been hiding all the time. They too had abandoned their cardigans. One of them was wearing a neon shiny tracksuit top and skinny jeans, and the other was wearing an oversized mohair jumper and leather trousers. (Which I think was a mistake, and not just because it was so hot. I mean, it's hot on stage even in the middle of winter because of all those lights shining on you. It's even worse at the beginning of July. The poor thing must have been boiling.) The audience cheered as the two boys leaped up on top of the packing cases, struck a pose and started to play.

'Wow,' I said. 'Niall really was paying attention during Shane's workshops.'

'Look, he's doing the "stretch out your hand to the crowd and then draw it back to your chest in a fist" move!' said Alice.

It was quite a show. I couldn't believe it was the same band who were mumbling away in their cardigans just a few weeks ago. Not that I have anything against cardigans. I actually LIKED their cardigans. In fact, I much prefer them to the tracksuit tops and the jumpsuits. I just thought the boys all looked the same when they were wearing them.

Anyway, they certainly all stand out now. And who knew Niall was such a showman? The only problem was that their music was still pretty boring. But you don't notice the boring-ness so much when they're all leaping up from behind boxes and pointing at the audience and stuff. Also, they'd even made a stage set! At one stage, the boys jumped off the packing cases and turned them around, and they'd painted a sort of backdrop and stuck it to the packing cases. It was of lots of pots of paint, and it took me a minute to figure out why, and then I realised the paint was all a sort of puce colour. Anyway, it looked quite good, and of course it made Cass say that she knew we should have had a set.

'We could easily have made a backdrop thing!' she said. 'It's just a couple of old sheets. No neon signs or anything. I'm definitely doing one for the next gig.'

I suppose we'll have to let her. She'll keep going on about it if we don't. And actually, it could be quite fun.

Unsurprisingly, Shane O'Driscoll was delighted by his protégés. When they finished – Niall stretched out his hand to the audience in a particularly impassioned fashion and then placed his hand on his heart – Shane jumped up on the stage and yelled, 'Let's hear it for my boys, Puce, the masters of stage craft!' And while that was going a bit far, we did give them a big cheer. After all, they'd put on an entertaining show. And they taught us that even if you can't afford actual trapdoors and stuff, you can get the same effect by hiding behind something and jumping out. Which is good to know.

Anyway, we didn't see Richard until Puce were over, so

when all the lights came on we all hurried to tell him and the rest of the Wicked Ways how good they were.

'The lying-down bit wasn't too much, was it?' said Richard.

'No,' I lied. Although maybe it wasn't a lie really. The show did all work in the end.

I was a bit worried that we'd see Charlie on the way out of the campus, but we didn't. We did see Evan, though. He looked pretty embarrassed, as well he might. But he nodded at us, and Cass nodded back.

'I know he's been an eejit,' she said. 'But he was pretty brave today, standing up to Charlie.'

'The world is upside down today,' I said.

And that's still what it feels like. But even though what Charlie said was horrible, and poor Cass was a bit wobbly all day afterwards, at least we found out that not everyone is totally evil. Even people I don't like very much. And that has to be a good thing.

THURSDAY ◎

Poor Jane! And poor Gemma and Josh and Alfie and Bernard

the Fairy-tale Prince. I even feel sorry for Karen, who has proved she is not totally evil. And maybe even Vanessa (okay, maybe not Vanessa). Their play was a disaster. Well, it wasn't so much that it was a disaster as that it didn't happen at all. It turns out that they hadn't told Cathy about all their special effects and knife-juggling and gymnastics and stuff, and when she heard about it this morning she was horrified and said the insurance wouldn't cover any of it so they couldn't do it. She asked if there was any way they could work around it, but they knew that if they took out all the controversial bits there'd only be about two minutes of play left so they had to cancel the whole thing.

I am surprised at how disappointed I am. I was looking forward to seeing whether Vanessa really could juggle with knives or not. Jane swears she is really good at juggling, but now we'll never know. I was actually tempted to ask Vanessa to give us a show, but I didn't dare. Of course, the whole group feel awful about not getting to put on the play. But Vanessa, unsurprisingly for a girl who has already thrown several tantrums in front of big crowds, was in a giant rage.

'I'll sue them,' she said furiously. 'I'll sue everyone in this stupid little so-called arts camp!'

'You do that, Vanessa,' said Karen loyally. 'We'll take them for every penny they've got!'

'I don't think that's a very good idea,' said Bernard nervously. 'I mean, we should probably have checked with Cathy about the fireworks. And the juggling. And the human pyramid. We just showed her the less ... action-filled bits.'

'Bernard's right,' said Jane sadly.

But Vanessa just kept on ranting on about knowing her rights and how she had lowered herself to come to what she called 'this crappy little camp' when she could have been at an international drama school in the Swiss Alps. (Jane told me later that actually, Vanessa couldn't have been in the Swiss Alps – her mum had told Jane's mum that Vanessa had been looking at the Swiss school's website, but it cost, like, a million euro a week, or something. I think Vanessa thinks her parents are richer than they actually are.) She also started going on about how she'd invited all those agents.

'This was my chance to be discovered!' she cried. 'And now no one will see my talent, thanks to that ridiculous fascist Cathy!'

This was too much even for Karen.

'But Vanessa,' she said gently, 'none of the agents turned up.

So it's not like they'd have seen you anyway.'

Vanessa clearly didn't have anything to say to this. She just made a sort of growling noise and stomped out of the room.

'Sorry you didn't get to do the show,' I said to Jane. Jane sighed.

'I suppose we should have gone through more stuff with Cathy,' she said. 'But she seemed so pleased we were working well together. It just seemed easier to ... skim over the dramatic bits. She thought it was a much shorter, sort of abstract piece.'

Poor Jane. It is such a shame after they worked so hard. She was so glum she didn't even cheer up when we went to see Positive Trigger and a few of the other bands do their show-case gig. I wasn't that excited about seeing Positive Trigger, because they've been rapping in the canteen every day for the last month so we know most of their songs already, but they were very good, especially Maggie's superfast rap about what goes on on the windswept Clontarf seafront, which, according to Positive Trigger, is some kind of gangster's paradise, even though whenever I've been there it's just full of middle-aged people walking pugs and Labradors.

And there was good news today too. First of all, it looks like we won't have to see Charlie again because he's not coming in to the camp for the last few days. In fact, he's basically been kicked out. Veronica and Tom found out about what happened yesterday, and this morning they talked to Cass, and they started asking around, and lots of girls – and boys – told them about the way Charlie's been acting all summer. Veronica and Tom were totally horrified and called his parents. And, according to Finn, who told Richard, they told Charlie that his behaviour was unacceptable, and if they'd known about it sooner, they'd have kicked him out ages ago. But all they could do was expel him for the last few days. We really should have gone and told them what he was doing instead of trying to ignore his creepy awfulness. In fact, Veronica and Tom basically said so this afternoon, before we went to the band showcase. 'We have a zero tolerance of bullying in this camp!' said Veronica, looking quite upset. 'But obviously we didn't make this clear enough. Just remember that if anyone is harassing you or making you feel scared, come and tell us or any of the other department facilitators and mentors straight away.'

If only we had. But at least he's been punished now. Apparently his parents are sending him to stay with his grandparents in a farm in the middle of nowhere for the rest of the summer, where there will be no humans to harass. So it seems that's the end of the Crack Parrots. I suppose it's hard on Evan and Finn, who did stand up to him in the end. But they put up with him for ages too, so it's not that unfair. And I bet they can start a new band. I mean, they were the best musicians anyway. Maybe the next time they'll find some bandmates who aren't total sexist homophobic goons.

And if they do, they might have a place to practise. Because Charlie getting expelled wasn't the only good thing that happened today. After Veronica and Tom told us about the no-bullying thing, they had an announcement to make.

'Over the course of the camp, one thing that's come up again and again is the difficulty of finding places to practise and to put on gigs,' said Veronica. 'So we thought we'd try and do something to help.'

And that means that they've managed to get the Knitting Factory to give over some of its studio space to keep the rock camp going at the weekends! We'll be able to bag a studio hopefully once a week. We'll still have to pay, but it'll only be about a fiver. And Veronica and Tom are going to put on regular underage gigs. So we'll definitely be able to play!

And that wasn't the only news. There's going to be a sort of disco on Friday night to celebrate the end of the camp, and we can take guests. So Cass is going to bring Liz along. Which is pretty cool. Oops, speaking of Cass, she and Liz and Alice are here for our epic sweet-making session. I'd better go.

LATER

We have made loads of fudge. And it is DELICIOUS. We have come a long way from that weirdly gritty first batch all those weeks ago. Having Liz helped – every addition to the team means we can get more speedy stirring done. We sang songs while we made it too, which Cass is convinced helped us stir faster. And we added some orange zest and juice to one batch for an extra kick. Anyway, it was definitely our best ever result, and even Rachel admitted that it tasted good. Though, being Rachel, she had to be rude about it.

'Are you sure you actually made this?' she said. 'You didn't buy it in some posh sweet shop?'

None of my family have any faith in my abilities.

We did have a bit of a problem with the boxes, though. We only made two of them. It turns out fashioning a box out of cardboard is more fiddly than it looks. By the time Cass had drawn out the template and painted it red and done the logo and Liz cut it out with a special craft knife she'd borrowed from her big sister (you're meant to do this on a special cutting board but we used the chopping board from the kitchen instead. I didn't tell Mum about this), and Alice glued it together, it was practically time for them all to go home.

So we decided that, for the moment, we're just going to put the fudge in clean plastic takeaway boxes with little Hey Dollface logos drawn on cardboard next to them and leave them out on the stage for people to help themselves. It is much easier all round. As Alice said, 'There's no point in overdoing it.'

I can't believe it's the last day tomorrow. I wish the camp was going on for another month.

FRIDAY ☺

It's over! The North Dublin Summer Arts Camp is over! And I feel a bit weird. And a bit sad. But also not sad, because ...

> 1. We made lots of friends, and we'll definitely see
>   them again. Well, actually, we'll see them again
>   in about an hour, because we're all going back

this evening for the disco/party in the Orchestra
Room.

2. We have a rehearsal space (more on this later).

3. We played a gig today and it was BRILLIANT.
And I didn't even fall off the stage.

But I'll start at the beginning.

Because it was the last day, we weren't having any workshops
at all. Instead, we were going to check out what everyone on
the other bits of the course had been doing. As soon as we got
into the arts building, Ellie ran up to us looking very nervous.

'Hey,' she said. 'Our art show's going to start in a minute!
Please come and say nice things about my stuff.'

We followed her into the art room where the exhibition was
taking place. It looked really impressive. There were different
sorts of artwork everywhere. Some people had done big oil
paintings; others had done tiny watercolours. Some had made
sculptures out of papier mâché and bits of metal; some had
created brilliant embroidered pictures. But we went straight to
Ellie's bit of the show. Which was amazing. All her designs for
the costumes were on display, and some of the actual costumes
were hung on the walls.

'Whoah,' said Cass. 'Ellie, you have come a long way from the days when you were Mrs Limond's slave.'

'Sorry you didn't get to see the costumes on stage,' said Alice, as we followed Ellie to the hall where the exhibition was taking place.

Ellie sighed. 'I know. I was looking forward to seeing how Gemma was going to do that cheerleading routine in the jumpsuit. It took me ages to make it. Still,' she brightened up a bit. 'It was fun making them. And really good practice. I've decided I'm not going to buy any clothes from now on. Apart from, like, knickers and bras and stuff. And maybe jeans. I'm going to make all my own stuff instead.'

'Wow,' I said. 'That's very cool.'

'Could you make stuff for other people too?' said Cass.

'Maybe,' said Ellie. 'I'll see how I get on.'

Sam and Lucy's comics were brilliant too. Especially Lucy's. Her pictures were all strange and spiky. She's definitely going to do more of the art in their joint comics from now on.

'I can't believe I left it so long to do all this drawing,' she said.

'And I'm going to write stuff too,' said Sam.

Truly this summer has broadened all of our horizons. And Lucy was still wearing her glasses. She says it's much more fun when she can actually see everyone's art work without putting her face right next to it.

Anyway, there was one last lunch in the canteen (I will miss that hideous place and its unflattering florescent lights. Okay, maybe not the lights). And then it was gigging time. We were all very excited, not just because we were going to play ourselves, but because Small Paula was on before us.

Of course, we were also looking forward to seeing Exquisite Corpse, who were up first. They were excellent, even though they're not my sort of thing musically at all. But they're such good performers. Tall Paula actually did do some prowling, which was very impressive. But at least we'd heard them before at various workshops. Small Paula's music was still a total mystery.

'At last, we'll get to see exactly what Small Paula's been doing all month!' said Alice, after Exquisite Corpse had left the stage to our enthusiastic cheers.

'I still think it's going to be all folky stuff, with some beats,' said Cass.

'I think it's going to be all ghostly and ethereal,' I said.

'I dunno,' said Alice. 'I still bet she sings like an opera singer.'

And then suddenly all the lights went out. A few people screamed, but then a deep voice – which belonged to Paula's mentor Dave – boomed out over the sound system.

'Welcome ... to the world ... of SMALL ... PAULA!'

And then suddenly the back of the stage was full of a big projection with the words SMALL PAULA in giant capital letters. And in front of it, in the middle of the stage, wearing her giant sunglasses and surrounded with keyboards and pedals and a laptop, was Small Paula herself. She was holding an electric guitar.

Cass, Alice and I stared at each other in amazement.

Small Paula hit a key on her keyboard, and a drum beat filled the air. Then she played a loud riff on her guitar and stood on a pedal, and the riff started playing again and again in a loop. She played a bassline on the keyboard, hit the pedal again, and the bassline kept playing. She kept doing this until there were loads of different bits of music all going at the same time. It was all very loud. It certainly wasn't all floaty and ethereal. And it wasn't folky either. It should have sounded like a mess, but it sounded ...

'Amazing!' whispered Alice.

She was right. And then Small Paula leaned towards the

microphone and started to sing. She didn't sound anything like her usual quiet voice. It was like a sort of beautiful roar. You couldn't even tell what she was saying, but it didn't matter. It was all really loud, and it should have all been just noise, but there was a tune in there somewhere. It didn't sound like anything I'd ever heard, but I knew I liked it. And as she played, strange but cool images were projected onto the back of the stage – foxes and other woodland creatures, and abstract shapes. It looked so cool.

'Small Paula is a genius,' I whispered to Cass.

'She's my new heroine,' Cass whispered back.

'And see how much she liked being called Small Paula!' I said. 'She's using it as her stage name!'

When she finished her first song, there was dead silence for a moment, and then everyone started cheering. Small Paula cracked a smile, just for a second. Then she just nodded and started the next song, which was as noisy and crazy and brilliant as the last one. She didn't say anything between songs, but that added to her mystique. In fact, by the time she finished her set to rapturous applause, everyone was so impressed by her we were really nervous about following her on stage.

'I think we might need more stage presence,' said Cass. 'I

mean, look at Small Paula! She was just standing there and not saying anything, but it didn't matter! I don't think we could pull that off.'

'I know,' I said. 'I knew I should have tried harder at being enigmatic and mysterious.'

'What?' said Alice.

'Nothing,' I said.

'We'll be fine,' said Alice firmly. 'Small Paula does her thing, and we'll do ours.'

And then we had to go and do it. Small Paula's equipment was taken off stage, Cass's keyboard and our extra microphones were taken on, our takeaway boxes of sweets with their little Hey Dollface signs were placed along the front of the stage, and then Kitty walked up to the mike and said, 'Hi, I'm Kitty, in case you don't know! And I'm very proud to welcome to the stage the brilliant ... Hey Dollface!'

'Okay,' said Cass. 'This is it.' She looked at me and grinned. 'Try not to fall off anything.'

'I'll do my best,' I said, took a deep breath, and walked onto the stage as the audience cheered. Luckily, my drum stool was on a nice flat bit of stage, and there was absolutely nothing to fall off. Which I have to admit did make me feel a bit better. I mean, you tell yourself lightning never strikes twice, but you never know. It would be just my luck to fall over again.

'Hello,' said Alice, looking straight out at the audience in a very confident, rock-star-ish fashion, just the way Kitty taught us. 'We're Hey Dollface. On guitar, I'm Alice Sheridan.' There was a big cheer. 'On keyboards, Cass McDermott!' And there was an absolutely huge cheer. Cass looked a bit embarrassed, but she couldn't help smiling. 'And on drums, Rebecca Rafferty!' There was quite a big cheer for me, not as big as Cass's, but I didn't mind really because all those people cheering her showed they were on her side, not horrible gay-hating Charlie. And then I did a big drum roll, and we started playing 'The Real Me', the first proper song we ever wrote, and everyone whooped and clapped.

I tried to remember everything we'd learned, from Kitty and from all the workshops. And as the song came together, it was like when we played at the Battle of the Bands, only better, because, after four weeks of rock camp, I really felt like I knew what I was doing. I stopped feeling nervous and just felt the music, and whenever I caught Cass's or Alice's eye I could tell they felt the same way. It wasn't scary at all. It was just ... fun. When we finished the first song and went into

'Ever Saw in You', as the John Kowalski song is now called, I felt so happy I almost laughed. And Cass was particularly brilliant. She's had that tendency to get nervous about playing, but she didn't seem nervous at all. She didn't even look down at her keyboard most of the time – she just fixed her gaze out on the audience like a total badass. She looked so cool.

I felt, no, I *knew* that we looked like a proper band. And we felt like one too. Our set was only five songs, but I didn't want it to end. It wasn't like we played the greatest gig ever – there were a few wonky notes, and once I nearly dropped my drumsticks. But the rest of the time, it was just really, really good. And the crowd seemed to like it, too. When we finished, there was another huge cheer.

'Thanks everyone!' said Alice. 'You've been a great audience. And to say thanks, we've made you some sweets! They're at the front of the stage, so help yourself.' Everyone cheered even more when they heard that. When we got off the stage, Kitty ran up and gave us each a huge hug.

'I'm so proud of you, ladies!' she said. 'You were brilliant.' She took a bite of orange fudge and looked quite startled. 'And surprisingly talented sweet-makers.'

She was brilliant too. We were really lucky to have her.

'And you've got to stay in touch now all this is over,' she said. 'I want to know how you're getting on.'

'You'll have to come to the Knitting Factory and see us,' said Alice, hopefully.

'You couldn't keep me away,' said Kitty.

'Aw, I'm going to miss Kitty,' I said, after we'd said our final farewell.

'I hope we'll remember everything she taught us,' said Cass.

'Of course we will,' said Alice. 'Look at Richard! I don't think he'll forget anything he learned from Ian Cliff.'

I caught Cass's eye for a second and then looked away. Much as we love Richard, and much as we like his outlandish stage antics, I think we both agreed that he has had enough of Ian Cliff for the moment.

And then Ian Cliff himself came up to us.

'That was really good,' he said. 'I especially liked the reference to a tercel in that "Ever Saw in You" song.'

'Really?' I said, amazed. 'That's brilliant. I didn't think anyone knew what a tercel was!'

'I'm a great admirer of birds of prey,' said Ian Cliff. And then he smiled. He looked a lot less intense and intimidating then. 'Keep up the good work, girls.' And off he went.

'Wow,' said Alice. 'I must tell Richard that Ian Cliff likes falcons and stuff. It might give him some inspiration for the new Wicked Ways songs.'

I suppose Ian Cliff is pretty nice, really. But I still think Richard has spent enough time with him for the moment. God knows what he'd be like if rock camp went on much longer. He'd probably start talking in his booming stage voice all the time. So to change the subject, Cass started talking about where to meet Liz before the party tonight. She isn't really nervous about Liz coming now, which is cool. So I'm going to meet all of them at the gates, and we'll go in to the party together.

Anyway, the whole course was pretty much over after the gig. Veronica and Tom came out and thanked us all for taking part, and we all gave them and the mentors a round of applause, and that was it. I felt a bit sad as we walked out the gates for the last time – I know it's not really the last time, because we're going back later. But we all knew it was the end of the course. It's been so much fun, despite Charlie. And just think, we'd never have known about it if it weren't for Vanessa and Karen. Who'd have thought they'd end up being the saviours of our summer?

SATURDAY ☺

I am very tired, but last night was so much fun. I met Cass and Liz at the gates, and when we arrived at the Orchestra Room I barely recognised it – there was a big glitter ball hanging from the ceiling, and there were fairy lights everywhere and a table with loads of crisps and fizzy drinks and stuff.

'Wow, this is amazing,' said Liz, as Alice ran over to get Richard, who was looking intensely at the crisps. (Alice says he finds choosing between snacks surprisingly difficult. He once spent ten minutes deciding between salt and vinegar Pringles and cheese and onion Kettle Chips.) 'Did it always look like this? Apart from the, you know, beverages and food and stuff.'

'No, it was usually much more boring,' I said. 'They've really gone all out!'

'Though it's not as fancy as the last big event we were at,' said Cass. 'Remember all the glitter at Vanessa's crazy Big Birthday Bash? I wish this party had a pink pony too.'

'Be careful what you wish for, Cass,' I said. 'It was that pony's fault that Alice broke her wrist.'

'Just fractured,' said Cass. 'Speaking of Alice, where is she?'

'Still helping Richard in his crisp choices,' I said.

'Hmm, there's Evan,' said Cass. 'You know,' she said to Liz. 'One of Charlie's band.'

'I hope he doesn't cause any trouble,' said Liz. She sounded a bit nervous, understandably.

'Well, he was the one who stood up to Charlie,' said Cass. 'So I think he'll be okay.'

And he was. In fact, he was more than okay. He came over to us, and although I felt a bit nervous when I saw him approach, I needn't have been. He looked even more nervous than I felt.

'Hey,' he said. He turned to Liz, who was holding Cass's hand tightly. 'Um, I'm Evan.'

'Hey,' said Liz.

Evan took a deep breath.

'I just wanted to say ... I'm sorry about Charlie. And the way he acted all summer. I should have ... I dunno. I'm sorry I didn't stand up to him more. Anyway, if it's any consolation, me and Finn have had enough of him. We're going to start a new band.'

'Ah,' said Cass. 'Thanks. Seriously, Evan. Thanks.'

'Cool,' said Evan. 'That's that. Um, your band were great today. And your sweets were really good. So ... I'll see you later?'

And he went off, looking very relieved.

'Wow,' said Liz. 'I think I need a nice cold drink. Or at least some crisps.' So we went off to get some.

The rest of the party was (mostly) brilliant. Veronica was the DJ, and she played really good music that you could actually dance to. (I know I have not been to many clubs – or any, in fact – but I hate when you're at a disco or a party, and they play a song that is good but not, like, funky, so everyone just ends up swaying around stupidly.) It was so much fun. At one stage, I looked around, and Cass and Liz and Alice and Richard were all grooving around to the old hip-hop song that Veronica was playing. Jane and Ellie were sort of acting out the lyrics, which was pretty funny. Nearby, Tall Paula and Small Paula were dancing together. It was almost a synchronised dance routine (one of my favourite things). Even Karen and Bernard the Fairy-tale Prince were dancing around and having a good time. And for a minute, I felt totally, perfectly happy.

But something happened later that made me feel a bit funny. And I feel weird that I felt a bit funny. If you know what I mean. Anyway, it happened towards the end of the night. I was talking to Cass and Ellie, and then Ellie said, 'Wow, look at Gemma and Sam. No, don't turn around, they'll see you!'

'Oh for goodness' sake,' I said. 'How can I look at them if I can't turn around?'

'Okay, you can turn around now,' said Ellic. 'But don't do it obviously.'

So I did. Gemma and Sam were near the stage, standing really close together, and she was sort of leaning towards him and smiling. And he was smiling back. And just as I turned around, she leaned over and started snogging him.

'Whoah,' said Cass.

And this is the funny thing. When I saw them kissing, I suddenly felt weird. Not like the time I saw Paperboy in town with a girl before we were going out and I thought she was his girlfriend. Not like that. That was terrible; it felt like having my heart wrenched out. This just felt ... really strange. Not jealous. Just weird.

Well, maybe a tiny bit jealous. I knew I didn't like what I was seeing. But why? I am actually amazed at my own feelings. I mean, I don't fancy Sam, do I? Of course I don't. I've had plenty of time to think about it. But I still didn't feel good when I saw him and Gemma all over each other.

'You can stop staring now, Bex,' said Cass. 'They might see you.'

And just at that moment, they stopped kissing, and Sam looked up and saw me staring at them. So of course I turned away and kept talking to the others. And I wasn't really talking to Sam much after that, which is a shame because I do really like him. As a friend. And I like Lucy. At the end of the night, we bumped into each other queuing for the cloakroom.

'Hey,' he said, smiling. 'Well done on the gig earlier, you were all great. And so was that fudge.'

'Yeah, you were brilliant!' said Lucy. She was wearing her glasses and bright red lipstick and looked really good.

'Thanks!' I said, trying to forget about my weird feelings earlier. 'Small Paula was a hard act to follow.'

'Yeah, wasn't she amazing?' said Sam. 'I didn't know she had it in her.'

'Me neither,' said Lucy. 'You definitely can't judge a book by its cover.'

Which is true. Lucy really is so nice. I can't believe I thought she was rude.

'I couldn't do it myself,' said Sam. 'You know how nervous I get about being in the spotlight. I had nightmares when I thought I might have to be John's understudy in the musical.' He shuddered.

'What about the art show?' I said. 'You were sort of in the spotlight then.'

'Ah, that was just my comics,' said Sam. 'It's different if it's me. Having a big light shone in my eyes is my idea of hell. Hey, speaking of hell ... did you finish that *Sandman* book?'

'Oh, yeah!' I said. 'It was brilliant! Though it was a bit scary. Actually very scary. But in a good way.' Then something struck me. 'Oh. I forgot all about giving it back to you. It's still at home.'

'Ah, don't worry about it,' said Sam. 'Sure, we'll all see each other over the holidays. Right?'

'Yeah, people are talking about going into town during the week, to the café at the Knitting Factory,' said Lucy as we reached the top of the queue. 'Maybe Wednesday?'

'Cool,' said Sam. He had got his coat now and was ready to go. 'Right, I'd better run, my lift is outside. See you then, Bex?'

'Oh yeah, definitely,' I said. And off he went.

And then Lucy said she'd started a Facebook group so we could all stay in touch – us and the Wicked Ways and Exquisite Corpse and Puce and Small Paula and the art kids and the drama gang. Basically all the nice people we've met at the camp. Which is great, so I suppose I'll see everyone on Wednesday. I hope Sam comes, otherwise I'll feel like a thief for keeping his book. And I can find out what's the story with him and Gemma. She's cool, so I hope she doesn't mess him around. He's so nice. Even though I don't fancy him.

Anyway! I have no time to think about him right now, because the showbiz magic never stops around here. Well, sort of. It is, of course, the first performance of *Oliver!* tonight. Mum and Dad seem a bit nervous, and who can blame them? I can't say I'm looking forward to seeing them humiliate (a) themselves and (b) me in front of the world (well, as much of the world as can fit into a primary-school hall, which is where the show is being produced). Cass and Alice are coming along for moral support, but I don't mind them seeing the show. They've seen my parents being embarrassing so many times, one more won't make any difference. And they're staying over afterwards – my parents don't often agree to big sleepovers, but they've been so distracted by their impending showbiz debut this week they'd have agreed to anything. I should really have taken more advantage of this and asked them for some more favours.

Anyway, they're not due until after six, so after the excitement and drama of the last few days, I will spend the day relaxing. I just saw Mrs Mulligan drive away with that stupid kid Sorcha in the back seat, so at least I know I won't be tormented by my enemy. After all, I need to build my strength before the performance – I have a feeling being in the audience as my parents prance about will be more stressful than actually performing on stage yesterday. I think I will go and have a nice lemonade to steady my nerves.

SUNDAY ☼

MY MIND HAS BEEN BLOWN.

And my world has been turned upside down. And it's all because of my parents and *Oliver!*. My parents were both so worked up about the show yesterday that they kept coming up with stupid chores for me to do (so much for my plans to spend the day relaxing and building up my strength). And for Rachel, of course, but she escaped to Jenny's house for a while in the afternoon. Anyway, at about six o'clock, after they had made some pizzas for a post-show treat (with my help, yet again I was forced to chop vegetables) and put them in the fridge, they went off to the school theatre to get ready for the show. So I could finally sit down.

But not for long, because soon Cass and Alice arrived to dump their bags.

'I'm quite looking forward to this,' said Cass. 'I like *Oliver!*.'

'Me too,' said Alice. And then they started singing 'Consider Yourself' very loudly until Rachel came in to see what all the noise was.

'Oh, it's you two,' she said. 'Are you coming to see our parents make a show of themselves?'

'It wouldn't be the first time,' I said.

'True,' said Rachel.

Anyway, we all headed down to the theatre together. I have to admit that I was quite intrigued myself. I mean, my parents have been going on about their musical skills for months, but, apart from their singing around the house, I'd never actually witnessed them in action. By the time we'd settled into our seats, though, I was feeling more nervous than excited. I mean, embarrassing as it all was for me, it would be worse for them if they made a total show of themselves. When the curtain went across, I caught Rachel's eye, and she made the sort of face that showed she was worrying about exactly the same thing. But we couldn't worry for long because, as Dad was playing the Beadle who runs the workhouse, he was in the very first scene.

'Oh God, here we go,' whispered Rachel, as little orphan Oliver (who wasn't very little at all, he must have been about fifteen, and he didn't look like he'd ever been starving in his life) walked up to the Beadle and asked if he could have some more food.

'More!' bellowed Dad, and I cringed. He did some more bellowing at Oliver before launching into the big song.

But then something happened. Dad was singing, and he was ... good. Like, seriously, really good. He stopped looking like an ordinary history lecturer from Drumcondra who was going a bit bald and started looking like an evil old Victorian Beadle, a Victorian Beadle with a very good deep singing voice. As he marched around the stage singing about all the terrible things he was going to do to Oliver, I almost forgot it was Dad.

'Woah, he's brilliant!' Cass whispered, but I barely heard her because, to my horror, the music had changed, and Dad was starting to dance.

'This wasn't in the film!' whispered Rachel, who sounded just as horrified as I was. But then I stopped feeling horrified because – and I can't believe I'm writing this – it turns out Dad really can dance. I mean, he can't dance on, like, a dance floor to pop music like a normal person. I have seen him at my cousin's party, and he was awful. But that's a different sort of dancing. This time he was dancing like, well, someone in a musical. He leaped. He twirled. He did some impressive tap dancing. He sort of glided across the stage. I wasn't even embarrassed because it was so obvious that he could really move. Daisy was right. He was poetry in motion!

I was so stunned by the whole thing I barely noticed what was happening in the next few scenes, though I could see Mum singing with great enthusiasm in the chorus.

As soon as the curtains closed for the interval, Rachel and I turned to each other in amazement.

'Did I just imagine that?' said Rachel.

'No, you didn't,' I said. 'He was brilliant!'

'He really was,' said Alice. 'I can't believe it. No offence to your dad, of course.'

'None taken,' I said. 'I can't really believe it either.' We were still in shock when the second half began. And then I got another surprise, because there was a scene where Nancy is singing in a pub, and Mum joined the actress playing Nancy and did a dance around the stage, and she was really good too! Not as impressive as Dad, but she was singing (very well) while waltzing around the stage, and, as I discovered when we were doing our own musical, it is surprisingly difficult to sing while you're walking, let alone dancing. When it was all over, we found ourselves joining in a standing ovation. The whole cast came out to take their bows, and Dad got an extra big cheer, especially when the director revealed that he was the understudy.

'Your parents should do this professionally,' said Cass. 'They're amazing!'

'Don't give them ideas,' said Rachel as our parents emerged, beaming, from backstage. But I could tell she was proud of them really. So was I.

'What did you think of my dance, girls?' said Dad, after we'd all told them how good the show was.

'I don't remember the Beadle doing that dance in the film!' said Alice.

'No, the directors added it in once they saw my moves,' said Dad happily. And I couldn't even mock him for referring to his 'moves' because those moves really were so good. 'Come on, let's go home and have that pizza.'

And so we did, and it was a lot of fun. We all ended up singing 'Pick a Pocket or Two' around the kitchen table – even Rachel, who generally acts like she's too grown up to do any messing. I suppose my family aren't that bad sometimes.

Anyway, it's the next day now, and Cass and Alice have gone home, and I am writing this in the back garden because it is lovely and sunny (for once). And even though I am all on my own because Cass is off with Liz and Alice is off with Richard, I am quite happy. It's nice to just laze around on your own sometimes, and I'll see them both on Monday at practice anyway. And, after what's happened recently, I'm not so worried anymore about my lack of love life. Daisy was right, everything else in my life is actually pretty good at the moment. And I'm sure I'll meet someone eventually. I mean, if my dad can turn out to be poetry in motion and Small Paula can turn out to be a noisy musical genius and Karen can turn into a heroine, then, really, anything can happen.

THE END

THE REAL REBECCA

My name is Rebecca Rafferty, and my mother has ruined my life. Again. I didn't mind her writing boring books for grown-ups. But now she's written one about an awful girl my age and everyone thinks it's me! Including the boy who delivers our newspapers, aka Paperboy, aka the most gorgeous boy in the whole world. Oh, the shame!

And if that wasn't awful enough, the biggest pain in my class wants to use my 'fame' to get herself on the reality show 'My Big Birthday Bash'.

I've just got to show everyone the REAL Rebecca. But how?

REBECCA RULES

1. My boyfriend has moved to Canada. Canada!
2. I have annoyed my best friends Cass and Alice by going on about him all the time.
3. I am going to a crazy girl's mad birthday party and I am not sure why.

Things have got to change. So I've made some new rules.

No moping.

No ignoring my friends' problems.

Find something exciting for me, Cass and Alice to do so our friendship gets back to normal.

Something fun. Something new ....

Something like joining the school musical.